Joe swerved to a stop at the end of the avenue of
trees. He got out of his car and ran towards the
indistinct outline of the van among the saplings.
Next moment, the van's motor was racing,
although no lights came on. It bucketed about on
the spruce needles for a moment, then began to
move forward.

'Mind what you're doing!' shouted Merrick,
staring in horror as Joe's shape became clear in
the headlights of his own parked car.

'Mind yourself!' replied Warne, and seemed
to aim the van straight at the running figure.
The hurtling vehicle hit Joe as he leaped out
of the way, and sent him sprawling among the
trees . . .

LEE MACKENZIE

Old Flames

Emmerdale Farm Book 17

Based on the successful
♥ Yorkshire Television series
originated by Kevin Laffan

FONTANA PAPERBACKS

First published by Fontana Paperbacks 1982

Chapter One

Incredible though it might seem, Jack Sugden was feeling something like gratitude to Richard Anstey. The manager of N.Y. Estates stood for all the things Jack hated in modern agriculture – fields the size of prairies for ease of tractor-handling, battery hens, hormone beef. Yet Richard Anstey had shown Pat Merrick an unexpected kindness, and for that Jack had to feel gratitude.

In order to get away from her wastrel of a husband, Tom, Pat had left Hotten to stay with an aunt on the outskirts of Beckindale. But Auntie Elsie was a widow-woman of unbending neatness; she didn't much care for teenagers with their casual ways and love of pop music. Cooped up with her in her little cottage, Pat's two children had reached the stage where they were becoming down-right rude to the old lady. Pat had tried everywhere to find accommodation, but the houses in and around Beckindale were either occupied or in use for holiday rental.

'Listen, Joe,' Anstey had said to Jack's brother. 'She can have that caravan in Lower Puddle Meadow, by Swinnow Wood, if it would do her for a bit. Nominal rent, of course – it's no great shakes as a home.'

Joe was a bit taken aback. He had put himself out a little to inquire for a flat or cottage, simply because he remembered how he'd felt when he was a teenager with an unsympathetic father telling him he'd better mind his p's and q's or he'd get a belting. But he certainly hadn't imagined N.Y. Estates would turn fairy godmother. A moment's thought showed him how it came about. Anstey believed that, as Jack was being very active in trying to help Pat, Jack's brother would be equally anxious. 'Little does he know,' Joe said to himself with grim humour. Pat was just one of the many points on which he and his elder brother didn't see eye to eye.

All the same, no reason why Pat and the two children

shouldn't have the caravan. He thanked Richard, came to an agreement about the rent to be charged, and passed the word to Jack.

Jack clapped him on the shoulder. 'Hey-up, our Joe!' he exclaimed, a beaming smile on his dark, thin face. 'That's a really kind-hearted act!'

'Not me. Richard.'

'Anstey?'

'Aye. Sitha, we're not all hard-faced financiers dragging dividends out of the soil, Jack. Richard's interested in the wellbeing of the whole community.'

'Good for him,' said Jack, although without great conviction. 'I'll stand him a drink next time I see him in the Woolpack.'

'I'll tell him.'

'When can she move in?'

'Any time – place is empty. We haven't used it since we had those extra hands to pick the trial bean crop. Mind, it's small, Jack. Got hot water by bottled gas, and there's electric cable led to it which we'll switch on when she moves in. All right?'

'Great!' enthused Jack, not put off by any little flaws his brother might be warning him about.

And when she heard about it, and was taken to see it, Pat was equally delighted. She ran her hands through her tawny brown hair and gave it a tug to show her delight. 'It's lovely, Jack!' she cried. 'There's really everything here we need –'

'Bit pokey, though –'

'Compact, that's what you call it,' she corrected. 'Look!' With delight she unfolded shelves, opened cupboards, switched the heater on and off though it was still unconnected to its electricity. She peered into the bedrooms, where the beds even had their pillows piled on them. There were curtains at the windows.

She twirled in the surprisingly capacious living room. 'It's gorgeous,' she declared. 'The kids'll love it!'

She was quite right. The delight of leaving Auntie Elsie, the pleasure of having a place of their own, blinded them to the drawbacks, of which there were several. One was that the caravan was in the middle of nowhere, which made it rather dark and spooky at nights to Sandie and Jackie, brought up in the town of Hotten. True, there was a path, but it had no lighting on it; it was a footpath which made a short cut to a lane which in its turn led down to Beckindale, and it was by this route that Pat and Sandie had to trudge with the household shopping.

Another drawback was that it was a little further to go to a pick-up point for the school bus to Hotten each morning. Jackie, never good at getting up, soon got fed up with being rousted out of bed with the refrain, 'Hurry up or you'll miss the bus.'

'If I had a bike I could go into Hotten on my own, Mum –'

'You've got a bike, Jackie.'

He groaned. 'I mean a proper bike, a motorbike. Only kids ride pushbikes.'

'Ho ho,' his mother said, making attempts to brush his hair as he gulped cornflakes. 'In the first place, where d'you think the money's coming from for a motorbike? And in the second place, you're not old enough to have a licence.'

'Yes I am. Sixteen's old enough.'

'Sixteen's old enough to have some sense,' his sister put in, giving him the look girls reserve for elder brothers who are being dense. Although he was two years her senior she often thought of him as her junior. Boys were so stupid. Surely he must realise they were only just making ends meet with Mum's job and Social Security? Motorbikes . . . It was like hoping for a hi-fi music centre and all the Presley albums. But at fourteen Sandie had already ceased to believe in miracles.

A miracle, for example, that would change their father Tom Merrick from a beer swilling, sullen layabout into a decent, sympathetic member of the community. Although Sandie had hated the breaking-up of their family, she understood it better than her brother. She could see how insensitive Dad had been, how demanding and deceitful. She too had grown sick of the continual promises to get and hold down a decent job, to do repairs and redecorations on their flat in Hotten, to stop knocking around with types in the local pubs who were apt to pick up things that had fallen off the back of a mythical lorry.

And yet ... And yet ... It was better to have a father, no matter how second rate, than no father at all. The other girls in Sandie's form would talk about their fathers in the course of conversation, not bragging, just taking them for granted. 'Dad says he'll come to the end of term play. Daddy won a prize at the rifle competition. My old man's a real terror when it comes to being home at night. Pop just doesn't understand about Barry Manilow, he just doesn't!'

Sandie had never been able to talk about her father in those terms, but it would have been nice to moan and criticise hers in the way the others did. As things were, she didn't mention Tom Merrick. Not even at home, where they all knew he'd been up in the magistrate's court for driving without a road fund licence and drunk and disorderly. Jackie mentioned him more than Sandie or her mother ... Which only went to prove, she sighed to herself as she went out for the walk to the school bus, that boys really are stupid.

If Annie Sugden sometimes shared this thought – that the younger members of the male species are not as sensible as they might be – she'd learned to keep the notion to herself. When she dropped in on her younger son to bring him a home-baked fruitcake, she wasn't surprised to find him making his evening meal off baked beans and fried eggs. She had an awful suspicion that these formed a large part of his diet.

'Why don't you come home more often for a proper meal?' she inquired mildly. 'You're always welcome, tha knows.'

'Aye, I know, Ma, but thing is, time's not my own any more. Often I'm the other side of N.Y. land when it comes time for food.'

'Working you hard, are they?' she inquired as she busied herself making tea to round off Joe's repast.

'Can't complain. Always the same on a new job, I

reckon. Got to learn, haven't I? And only way to do it is to *do* it.'

'I suppose so.' She warmed the teapot, cupping it in her hands. 'Think you're going to like it?'

Joe's new job as assistant manager of N.Y. Estates was still a source of wonder at Emmerdale – and indeed in the surrounding area. It had always been taken for granted that Joe would go on at Emmerdale, improving the farm where he could and getting the best financial return out of what couldn't be altered. Perhaps it would have been so if Jack had not come back from Rome to settle back into a farmer's life. Joe had too much sense of responsibility ever to leave Emmerdale Farm without someone who knew how to guide the plough. But, in effect, Jack's return had set Joe free to go out after the new world of agriculture – what Jack chose to call 'agri-business', farming on a large scale. Joe's short trip to America had shown him what could be done with the land if machines and new methods were employed: it would have been impossible to try these out at Emmerdale but he had jumped at the chance to learn these new ways in his job with N.Y. Estates under Richard Anstey.

'Some of the things are downright intricate,' Joe told his mother. 'Working out wage dockets, you know – so much deducted for tax and Social Security, so much added on at such a rate for overtime and special skills.' Joe chuckled. 'Special skills! Fancy paying Matt extra for special skills! It never even occurred to me, Ma. Yet it's current practice in a business like N.Y. Estates.'

Annie looked thoughtful and poured tea into two mugs. 'Happen we haven't valued Matt's abilities properly.'

'You can say that again!' Joe agreed. 'If Matt ever decided to move on, he'd make twice what he does at Emmerdale. But luckily he isn't likely to do it 'cos he's a shareholder. That holds him to Emmerdale.'

'Oh, Joe,' Annie said with a hint of reproof, 'I hope it's more than his share in the business that keeps Matt with us.'

'Of course. I didn't mean that. I was just pointing out ...' He paused, sipped his tea, and gazed at the electric fire. 'See how I'm beginning to analyse things now? I don't believe it ever dawned on me to think along those lines when I was boss at Emmerdale. Day to day living seemed to take up every available minute. Now I delegate the actual work to other folk, I have a chance to stand back a bit and see what makes it all tick.'

She gave a little smile. 'And what, in your opinion, makes us tick at Emmerdale, Joe?'

'Huh? That's a good question, Ma. I reckon you stay there because you belong there and it belongs to you, in a way. You fit together. Jack's there because he's retreating from a life he found disappointing and empty – and because for time being, he's run out of summat to write. Matt and Dolly are at Emmerdale because he happened to marry into the family years ago and now he's inherited Peggy's share – and besides, he's loyal above everything. Henry . . . Henry "ticks" because he chose to come here and make a new life in his retirement. He wasn't running away from owt – he made up his mind to start again and by jingo, he's done it. So there you are.'

Annie was quite taken aback. 'You've really thought about it, Joe.'

'Oh aye. There's a process in business called "decision-making". It's interesting to try and work out how people come to decisions. I've put my mind to that kind a lot over the past few weeks since I started at N.Y. Estates. And,' – he laughed – 'if you want to know, seems to me that even the most important business decisions are made on a momentary impulse! You weigh things up and you think Yes I'll do it or No I'll not do it. But at the moment you have to announce your decision, any of a hundred things can influence you – state of weather, whether you have a hangover or not, whether you're speaking to someone you like or hate . . . All that. For instance . . .'

'What?'

'Pat Merrick. I bet she made up her mind a hundred times to leave Tom, but changed it at the last minute because . . . oh, because she hadn't got enough ironing done to get the kids' clothes ready, or because it was

Jackie's birthday coming up and she didn't want to spoil it, or something of that kind.'

'But she's done it at last, poor lass. It's no joke, lad, trying to fend for yourself and two children on your own – let alone with a husband like Tom Merrick always likely to pop up and make a nuisance of himself.'

'Been doing that, has he?'

'He's around in the village,' she murmured. 'I've seen him myself, and other folk mention him. What's he doing here? If he's seriously looking for a job, he stands more chance in Hotten than in Beckindale.'

'A job? Tom Merrick? That'll be the day,' Joe snorted. 'Happen he wants to keep contact with his kids, though, Ma.'

'You mean he's suddenly turned into a "concerned parent"?' she replied with some dryness. 'He had sixteen years for that. Bit late to start now, isn't it?'

Joe laughed and collected up his dirty plates. 'I'll just wash these up and then I'm off out, Ma.'

'Seeing Judy Westrop?'

He sighed and shook his head. 'Nay, it's a sort of business meeting with a couple of blokes in Connelton, about showing our game-keeping methods at t'next Gamekeepers' Fair. Never have time for girls these days, Ma. And to tell truth, Judy doesn't have time either. That estate agent job's keeping her busy.'

'Maurice wrote from Wales last week. Seems he's doing well. He said he'd made a contact for Judy with a big agency in Cardiff. I got the notion Judy might take it up.'

'Oh aye?' Joe said without undue concern, which told his mother what she wanted to know – that he wouldn't be breaking his heart if Judy left. But then Judy had always been more keen on Joe than he was on her.

Next morning Joe had the usual routine visits to make around the estate. He distributed the pay envelopes to the men, stopping for a chat wherever any of them seemed to have something to say. Already Joe had learned that it paid to keep your senses alert for any complaints before

11

they got to be important. Daniel, the cowman, kept him for some time arguing against the notion of using hormones on a large scale at Ridge Farm, where the experimental beef unit had been set up. Now that was a topic that might cause some concern if Richard decided the figures justified a fullscale investment.

Having a moment to spare, Joe decided to drop in on Emmerdale. His mother's visit the previous evening had made him realise he was something of a stranger there at present. He was amazed as he took his Land-Rover down the familiar lane to see his brother Jack edging to and fro on the four-acre with the plough on the tractor.

With an amused frown, Joe drew up and got out. He sat on the stone dyke until Jack, on one of his turns, noticed him. The tractor was switched off and after a moment Jack, looking a bit pink, got out of the tractor cab. 'Hello, Joe,' he called as he walked over.

'What on earth were you doing?' Joe inquired. 'Learning the foxtrot?'

'Er ... well ... as a matter of fact, I was trying to get the hang of a neat turn on the headland so as to get the line absolutely straight when you start again.'

'Since when has it mattered too much about how untidy your turn is?'

'Er ... em ... Fact is, I'm thinking of going in for the ploughing competition at Loudwick Show next month.'

'You never are!'

'Yes, I am,' Jack insisted. 'What's wrong wi' that?'

'Nothing at all, except that you haven't handled a plough for more than about six months after an absence of about twelve years. If you really think you can get the knack in three weeks, you've another think coming.'

Jack suddenly grinned. 'You're right, of course. But I suddenly got the urge to try. No harm in that, is there?'

'I suppose not.' Joe hesitated, about to remark that there were other and more important things his brother ought to be giving his mind to if he were going to take farming seriously, but held his tongue. A few weeks experience at N.Y. Estates had already taught him the value of keeping his peace. 'I'll come and watch you give your display,' he promised. 'How's things otherwise – apart from the knotty problem of how to turn on a sixpence?'

'Not bad, I s'pose. Matt's got some good ewes coming up for showing, and we've booked a hotel for whoever goes down to Smithfield this year, Dolly's getting really involved with that play-group work, and I've given up trying not to hear the alarm at five-thirty.'

'Heard that there's a bit of unrest among Mitchelson's drivers? There may be a go-slow on feed deliveries.'

'Oh, that. I heard it was settled.'

'Hope so. What are you putting in twenty acre for next year?'

They began a discussion of the merits of clover and barley as they wended their way to the house for mid-morning coffee. Annie was pleased to see her younger son. Her visit of the previous evening had contained no complaint of his neglect yet all the same he had got the unspoken message – that he was missed, that she wanted to see him.

His grandfather gave a grunt as he took a seat at the kitchen table. 'Oh, got a spare second to drop in on us, have you? I'm surprised.'

'Now, Grandad, don't be like that. You know I told you I'd buy you a cider in the Woolpack any time you cared to drop by.'

'Comes to things when I have to make appointments to see my own grandson in the local pub!'

'Dad, will you clear that stuff off the table, please?' Annie put in. 'I want to put the plates and mugs out.'

'But I've got to give these a rub up, Annie. No good wasting time carving them if you don't treat the wood so the grain shows.'

Joe picked up one of the little animals his grandfather was working on. It was a perfect representation of an ox, kneeling. The figures were for the Crib in Beckindale Parish Church at Christmas. Sam carved a set each year, which were afterwards given to an orphanage in Hotten. 'That's real champion, Grandad,' Joe said. 'Nice bit of wood.'

13

'Aye, rosewood, is that. Just happened on it – in the back of the shed.'

'Oh, there's treasure in the back of that shed,' Matt said, coming in from the yard bringing with him the scent of disinfectant. He took off his overall coat, hung it on the hook by the door, divested himself of his gumboots, and went to wash up for his coffee. 'I've finished cleaning up the calfbox,' he announced. 'Millicent can bring t'new one into t'world any time she likes now.'

'How's she doing?' inquired Joe.

'All right. Jack and me's got a bet on. I say it'll come night after tomorrow. Jack says it'll be tonight.'

'I'll put my money with yours,' said Joe. 'You're seldom wrong.'

'Aye, and calving's not the only thing Jack's wrong about,' Sam muttered, keeping his eyes fixed on the wood he was rubbing.

Annie coloured a little and Jack looked vexed. No one said anything, but they all knew he was referring to Jack's friendship with Pat Merrick which, though now slight, had caused eyebrows to be raised.

How true it was Joe had no idea, but it was widely believed in Beckindale that before he left his home all those years ago, Jack Sugden had had an affair with the girl who later became Pat Merrick. In fact there were those who said Pat had married Tom Merrick to give a father to the child who by rights belonged to Jack Sugden. Sometimes, catching sight of Jackie Merrick in the village, Joe would think there was a likeness to his elder brother. But when you came down to it, it consisted of the fact that they were both dark-haired and brown-eyed and rather tall and slim.

It was certainly a fact that Sam didn't like the gossip. He wanted Jack to avoid Pat Merrick or, better yet, he wanted Pat Merrick to leave Beckindale and go back to her husband like a respectable married woman.

Jack Sugden was well aware of his grandfather's views. Sam used every opportunity to get his digs in about Pat. But that didn't have the effect he desired. Quite the contrary. Jack was never going to let it be said that his grandfather ruled his life. Besides, he liked Pat. It had given him real pleasure to see her again when she came back to Beckindale at about the time he returned for good.

He could quite easily have gone to some other cafe in Hotten on market day but no – he chose to go to the one where Pat had a part-time job. The place was busy, because market day was Saturday in Hotten and the town was full of shoppers too. Jack got himself a cup of tea, telling himself it didn't really matter whether he saw Pat or not.

By and by she came along to clear used crocks from the side table where he was sitting. 'Hello, Jack. Thought you'd be after summat stronger!'

'That comes later. I'm meeting Matt and Dolly for a ploughman's lunch when they've finished buying up the stores. How're you, Pat?'

'Not bad. You?'

'The same.' Not for anything would he have pressed for information, yet he longed to know what had happened in her life. Some weeks ago she had asked Jack to recommend a solicitor for help in a 'private matter'. Jack knew of only one solicitor, the man who handled Emmerdale affairs. He gave her the name and address but nothing more had been said.

She wiped the plastic surface of the table with a damp cloth smelling of washing-up liquid. 'Had you anything in the market this morning?'

'Nay, just came in to get an idea of prices and to put in an order for feed – there's some sort of a hold-up on that. And Dolly wanted to show Matt some spinning equipment. You know she's into spinning her own wool from our sheep?'

'Fancy that! What's she showing it to Matt for – this equipment?'

Jack grinned. 'Ah, Pat, that shows you're not well up on feminine wiles! She wants Matt to buy it for Christmas.'

Pat said nothing. She turned her head away, but he could see in the downward curve of her mouth the reaction to this little joke about husband-and-wife relationships. He put his hand over hers on the table, damp cloth and all. 'Pat love, I'm sorry.'

She drew her hand away, refolded the cloth, hesitated, then said: 'You know that lawyer?'

'Mr Jones – aye?'

'He was ever so nice. Talked to me for a long time and took it all on himself. He went along with me when I had to appear –'

'Appear?'

'Marital Causes Board. I were applying for a legal separation.'

'Oh. I didn't know.'

'It's so Tom can't keep coming pestering. He can make life very difficult.'

'I can imagine. What did he say at the hearing?'

'Nowt. He didn't show up. Mr Jones explained he'd had little or no reaction from him and they decided in my favour wi'out too much discussion. Custody of the kids though he has the right to visit them with my agreement.'

'I suppose you keep it as few visits as you can ... '

'So far he's been twice, by arrangement. But I have an awful feeling he sneaks around when I'm not there, Jack.'

'Can't do that too much, can he, Pat? The kids are at school most of the time.'

'I know.' She sighed. 'It's just a feeling I have. Jackie comes out with things sometimes – sounds just like his father speaking.'

She stood half-turned away, dejected. Jack waited a moment then said in an optimistic tone: 'Still, never mind, eh? Look on the bright side. You're legally free of him to a certain extent and you've got a place to live and a bit of a job. And the kids are doing well at school, I expect.'

'Sandie is. She's bright, you know. But Jackie ... I dunno ... He doesn't take much to country life, you see. Funny, that – Hotten is hardly the big city but he seems to like streets and cafes more than meadows and woods. I don't know as he'll ever make a countryman.'

16

'Tell you what – how about coming with me to Loudwick Agricultural Show at the end of the month? Sideshows and craft-stalls as well as buttermaking exhibitions. And the greatest exhibition of all will be me.'

'You?'

'I'm entering for the ploughing competition.'

'Good for you,' she said. It didn't occur to her to laugh at the idea. Pat had been away from Beckindale as long as Jack, almost. She didn't realise how out of practice he was at the art of the ploughman.

'Mrs Merrick!' called a cross voice from the serving hatch. 'If you can spare a moment, I need those cups and saucers you're supposed to be clearing.'

Pat raised her eyebrows and made a little moue of resignation. 'Her master's voice. I better go.'

'But how about the Show, eh?'

'I'll see what the kids say, Jack. Thanks for the thought.'

She hurried away, carrying her laden tray of used cups and saucers. Jack looked at his cold tea, frowned, got up, and went out. Not much of a life for her, working for someone who shouted criticism across the whole cafe. But then jobs were scarce in and around Beckindale. Pat probably thought herself lucky to be employed at all.

When Pat got home to the caravan that evening, very tired after a hard day's work in a crowded cafe, she found an argument in progress between her son and her daughter. That was about par for the course, these days. There seldom seemed to be tranquility between them.

'What now, you two?'

'He won't help get the tea, Ma. He just sits there reading his pop music mag and listening to his transistor.'

'I did the taters,' Jackie complained.

'Oh yes, big deal, peeled more off than he left on –'

'Well, you were using the peeler on the carrots –'

'But you said you could do better with a knife – the big white-hunter type –'

'I never said that, I said men had been using knives a lot longer than tittupy little peelers –'

17

'They don't use peelers or do any jobs if they can help it, if you ask me –'

'Will you be *quiet*!' exclaimed Pat, surprising herself by the vehemence of her own voice.

The two youngsters drew back and turned to stare at her. At once she was sorry she had shouted at them. It wasn't their fault they were edgy. Children without a father, and in a skimpy little rented home . . .

'Put the kettle on, love,' she said to Sandie. In silence her daughter obeyed. A little current of sympathy flowed between them.

'Did you get my paper?' Jackie inquired.

Pat drew this week's *Melody Maker* from her shopping bag. Her son seized it, opened it, and began to read it with avidity. Sandie said sharply: 'Don't spread it all over the table, Jackie. I'm just going to put tea on.'

'Aw, the vegetables aren't cooked –'

'Yes they are, nearly, and besides, have you ever heard of forks and knives?'

'Now, you two,' Pat said. She began taking groceries from her shopping bag and putting them away. Over her shoulder she said to her son: 'Don't read it now, Jackie. Help your sister lay the table.'

'Eh?' said Jackie from behind the pages.

'I said put it down, Jackie.' With a sigh of martyrdom he obeyed. Pat went on: 'Any road, I want to talk. What have you been doing today?'

The boy shrugged. 'Not much.' He opened the drawer in the sink fitment and took out cutlery which he began to throw on the table at the approximate spot where it would be needed. 'Stephen Jelks came along for a bit. He's got a one-two-five.'

'A what?'

'A motorbike, Mum. It's smashing. He took me for a ride on the pillion –'

'What! Aren't you supposed to have a crash helmet if you ride on a bike?'

'He brought a spare, Mum,' Jackie soothed. 'It was great. Sandie wouldn't go on it. She was scared.'

'I was not,' interrupted Sandie. 'I had homework to finish, and so had you.'

At this betrayal her brother flashed her a look that ought to have singed her eyebrows. She had the grace to look ashamed.

'You can do it tonight, Jackie,' said Pat. 'Look, I bought some bourbon biscuits – we can have tea and bourbon biscuits about eight o'clock, when you've finished.'

Such treats had once had the power to coax Jackie into settling down to work. But he had grown out of them. 'Oh Mum,' he groaned.

'It's got to be done, Jackie. If it's not done tonight you'll only have to do it tomorrow. You don't want to spend Sunday indoors doing homework, now do you?'

'Don't see why not. There's nowt else to do around here.'

'Listen, the pair of you,' Pat said, trying for brightness. 'We're going to have a day out at the end of the month. What d'you think of that?'

'A day out? Where? We going to Leeds?'

'No, there's an Agricultural Fair at Loudwick –'

'Oh, *no*,' groaned Jackie.

'But you'll like it, love. Sideshows an' all –'

'It sounds like Hicksville.'

'He's always the same,' Sandie remarked with indignation. 'Nothing's any good unless it's to do with pop music or cars or bikes or space movies –'

'Oh, I suppose you think algebra and geometry are a lot more fun –'

'I'll tell you this, your hero Lance Skywalker or whatever his name is could never have got off the Earth if it hadn't been for algebra and geometry –'

'That's enough!' Pat cried. 'That's more than enough. I'm going to have a sit down and a cup of tea, and I don't want another word about bikes or anything else. And that homework's going to be done this evening or there'll be no television. Straight after we've eaten, right, Jackie?'

'All right,' he muttered, hearing the voice of authority.

'And we're going to have a day out at Loudwick

19

Agricultural Show with Jack Sugden and I don't want to hear any clever remarks about Hicksville.'

'Jack Sugden?' her son echoed, his dark brows coming together.

'He's kindly invited us to go and I've accepted. It's very nice of him.'

'I'm sure,' Jackie said under his breath, taking a bottle of sauce from the cupboard and slamming it on the table.

His mother watched Sandie making the tea with deft movements. Of course a daughter is always more of a comfort to her mother, she thought, or at least so the saying goes. . . . Why did Jackie have to be so difficult?

And why did he always go so quiet when Jack Sugden's name was mentioned?

Chapter Two

Joe was beginning to understand what were the main problems in running a big concern like N.Y. Estates. Anstey called on Joe for his opinion frequently, not only on matters of agriculture on which he had special knowledge of the terrain, but on management. Soon after Joe took on the job, there had been mutters of discontent among the men about pay, which came to Joe's ears because he was always careful to stop and listen.

The long and short of it was, the men wanted to unionise. Anstey was quite upset about it. 'It's as if they don't trust us to be fair with them unless they have a union here . . .'

'I don't see why you're letting it bother you, Richard. We're paying union rates and above as it is. They won't do much better with a trade union negotiator, and they'll soon find that out.'

'But it makes for bad feeling –'

'Not if you just tell 'em the facts. That Ian Reeve is a decent enough bloke – he doesn't want to jack up wages so that he puts his own members out of jobs.' Joe had had a drink or two with Reeve in Connelton and in Harrogate, at farming events. He didn't think there was much to fear from him. But of course, Joe didn't carry the responsibility that lay on Anstey's shoulders.

'How're we doing, any road?' he enquired. 'You're getting figures together for an end-of-year report to head office, aren't you?'

'I'd say we're not quite breaking even. By my reckoning it'll be another two years before the books balance, and maybe another twelve-month before we start to show a profit.' He smiled wryly. 'I don't suppose I'll still be here then.'

'You what?' Joe said in surprise. 'How come?'

'Oh, it's the career structure of a business like N.Y. I should think I'll have moved on by then.'

Joe was struck to silence. He still wasn't used to the idea of mobility. The notion that you simply upped stakes and moved on every few years was not exactly displeasing, but it was strange. He couldn't quite come to terms with it.

The arrival of the trade union organiser put a stop to these reflections. An amicable talk was carried on between the three men. Anstey tried to put his point about the viability of N.Y. Estates as a business but Reeve had done his homework. 'You're part of a big combine that's in profit elsewhere, Mr. Anstey. I don't intend that my members should suffer just because they happen to live in the Dales. Your company can finance the increase in wages from other sectors, and they know it, and I know it. So we'll negotiate on that basis if you don't mind.' His tone was rather stern, but he favoured Joe with a wink from the eye on the side of his face that was turned away from Richard Anstey.

Joe knew they would come to an agreement without too much trouble, and so it proved. Reeve carried his point about increased pay over special tasks involving safety, and here he especially emphasised the hormone treatment for beef cattle. 'But there's no danger, Mr. Reeve,' Anstey began.

'So you say, but there's no long-term scientific work on that. Come to me in fifty years and say it doesn't harm the cowman to be handling meat-enhancing hormones, and I'll believe you. But just at present, I want your stockmen to get an allowance for taking on the work.'

When they had argued enough to justify their different outlooks and noted a few figures on sheets of paper, Reeve accepted a drink, shook hands, and left in search of his midday meal.

'That was better than you expected,' Joe remarked.

'Yes, it was. But I do wish folk'd get rid of this absurd bias against modern farming methods.'

'The hormones, you mean?' Joe shrugged. 'If it wasn't that, it'd be summat else. Remember all that fuss about the hedge we took out between Mitchelson and Rye Loom? You'd think the end of the world was coming. But it died away.'

'The fuss over battery hens and veal calves doesn't go away, though.'

'No-o. But things like that take time. Any road, I think you did a good job on the pay issue. He'll refuse to go lower, you'll tell head office and they'll say it's astronomical, you'll both move towards each other a bit, and Reeve'll end up taking what you had in mind in the first place. That's how it's done, isn't it?'

'You catch on quick,' Anstey grinned. 'Another?'

'No, thanks, think I'll drive over and see how my mother's getting on.'

'Anything wrong?'

Joe frowned. 'Dunno. She had to go for an X-ray yesterday.'

Anstey paused in the act of pouring himself another glass of sherry. 'An X-ray? That sounds . . . '

'Oh, it were only on her knee,' Joe explained hastily. 'I say "only" – seems she's been having a lot of pain in it for some time but never let on. Any road, she went and had the X-ray yesterday and she's to go back again some time next week to hear what they think should be done. Thought I'd just drop in and ask if she got any hints yesterday.'

'So long then. See you at Ridge Farm by two-thirty, eh?'

'You what? Was that an arrangement?'

'Didn't I mention it to you? This thing with Reeve put it out of my head, I s'pose. Yes, I want you over there while the light's still good, Joe. I'm going to introduce you to the mysteries of forestry.'

Joe looked at him in surprise. 'That's news to me. I know nowt about it.'

'Never too late to learn, Joe.'

'That's true. And of course I'm anxious to learn all I can.'

'All right, then, two-thirty. See you.'

Joe drove off not quite sure why Richard Anstey should have been suppressing a smile during that last exchange.

Once again as he neared Emmerdale Joe witnessed his brother doing waltzing revolutions with the tractor and plough. This time Sam Pearson was leaning against the stone wall at the field's edge, watching him.

'How do, Grandad,' Joe said, joining him and surveying Jack's furrows. 'What d'you think, then?'

Sam gave a snort. Jack, at the far end of the field, turned and came back. Sam walked forward a few paces, stooped, eyed the line of the tractor's advance, straightened, and signalled with a wave of his arm that Jack was off to the right. Amused, Joe watched and waited.

Inevitably Jack swerved too far to the left at his grandfather's warning. He finished the furrow, stopped, switched off, and jumped out of the cab. He walked round the tractor to survey the results.

'I made a big kink there,' he sighed.

'Aye.'

'That was when you signalled to me?'

'Aye.'

'Made a poor job of it.'

'Aye.'

'Oh,' said Jack. 'Bad as that is it?'

'No use beating about the bush, Jack. If you go into the competition you'll be competing against Bob Potts from Garsdale, Wally Mabers of Leeming – I wonder if you

23

know what you're up against?' He turned to Joe. 'Tell him, Joe.'

'Very artistic, is that,' Joe opined. 'I hear tell they're on to it in California.'

'On to what?'

'Landscape art. They go out with ploughs and bull-dozers and that, draw designs on the ground, circles and diamonds and so on.'

'Oh, very funny. It's only a little bit squint.'

'That's what I'm saying, lad,' Sam told him. 'Wally Mabers never ploughs a little bit squint.'

'Tell you what, though,' Joe put in. 'This field is being ploughed wi' more thoroughness than it ever got afore!'

Laughing, they went into the lane and up the rise to the farm. Annie and Dolly were at work getting the midday meal. 'You staying for dinner, Joe?' asked Annie.

'No thanks, I've got to be over Ridge Farm by half-two, and I've got other things to do before then. Just dropped by to hear about yesterday.'

'There's nowt to tell, lad. They took me into a room in the basement, laid me on a sort of high table, took three pictures, and went off to develop them. When they were satisfied the pictures were clear, they told me that was all and I could go.'

'You seeing the specialist next week – is that right?'

'Aye. It's nowt, really. He'll give me some embroca-tion, I reckon.'

Joe hung around long enough to cadge a cup of coffee and tease Jack about his prowess as a ploughman. Later in the day Jack went to the caravan to confess to Pat that he had decided to withdraw from the ploughing competi-tion. 'But we can still go to the show, you know,' he urged.

'Well . . . tell the truth, Jackie doesn't seem all that keen on the idea. He thinks it's . . . I dunno . . . dull.'

'Oh,' said Jack. Then, after a moment, 'Perhaps he's right. Tell you what, if it's a nice day let's go somewhere special – drive somewhere and have a picnic. How about that?'

'Oh, that would be lovely,' she exclaimed, relieved that

the prospect of a day away from the caravan was not to be snatched from her. 'Where shall we go?'

'Somewhere where we can go indoors if it rains, eh?'

She was going to say 'York', for there was the railway exhibition there, sure to interest a boy. But Jack came out with 'Harewood House?'

'Oh yes, I've never been there. I hear it's lovely.'

'Okay then, that's a date. I'll get Ma to do some things for the picnic –'

'No, no, I'll see to that –'

'Nay, it's no trouble to Ma –'

'But you're giving us this day out, it's up to me to provide the eats –'

'Tell you what, you bring something and I'll bring something – what d'you say? You bring the sandwiches and I'll bring the cake.'

'It's a deal.'

It occurred to neither of them that if an Agricultural Show wasn't Jackie's idea of fun, Harewood House was hardly likely to send him into raptures.

Jackie made his displeasure felt when they set out that Sunday. Offered the front seat next to Jack, he shrugged and climbed in the back of Annie's car, which Jack had borrowed for the occasion. Sandie, anxious to smooth over any difficulty, immediately climbed into the passenger seat and they drove off. On the drive she kept up polite conversation about the scenery and her school-work; for some reason she could never understand, grown-ups always wanted to talk about your schoolwork. But as it happened she was in the middle of a project for Christmas connected with the possible origins of the legend of the Star of Bethlehem.

'It wasn't Halley's comet, you know.'

'It wasn't?' he queried gravely.

'No, couldn't have been, it only occurs every seventy-five or seventy-six years and if you calculate back from 1910 when it last appeared you can see it couldn't have been the Star.'

A grunt from the back seat told of Jackie's reaction to the idea of calculating seventyfives into two thousand years. Sandie turned in annoyance and addressed him over her shoulder. 'I'd have thought even you would see that there's some value in being able to handle figures, if it can tell you an interesting thing like that.'

'Depends what you mean by interesting,' muttered Jackie.

'Interesting' certainly didn't mean the architectural pleasures of Harewood House. The almost total silence of the eight miles drive from Leeds was broken by a snort of boredom at the great Adam facade, and a few more snorts as they joined the group being escorted through the displays of Adam and Chippendale, the Sèvres porcelain, and the galleries of old masters.

Pat dropped back to take him by the arm. 'Come on now, Jackie, try at least to show some interest.'

'But I'm *not* interested!'

'You're making that only too plain. Whatever happened to good manners?'

'I didn't want to come. You dragged me here.'

'I thought you'd like a nice drive and a chance to see something different . . . '

'What's different about a load of old furniture? There isn't even a safari park –'

'There's a bird garden –'

'Huh! I suppose we'll get to that after we're worn out looking at cups and saucers and shepherdesses!'

Pat gave up. Someone who is determined not to enjoy himself is hard to coax. But when they came to an open set of french windows Jackie said in Sandie's ear, 'I'm off' and, dropping back from the group, stepped through into freedom. The gardens were beautiful. In the crisp cool sunshine of early November the trees were dark gold and umber touched with brown where the bare branches peeped through. He walked down a path, round a hedge, down steps with ornamental urns alongside – and heard the cry of a peacock.

Startled, he stopped. A strange, eerie call. A ghost? He set off to track it down, and came across the stately bird pacing across a lawn beyond which were enclosures where green wings fluttered in the sun.

He had found the bird garden.

Against his will, Jackie was interested. When he had mourned the absence of a safari park, there had been genuine regret besides a wish to annoy his elders. He genuinely liked animals, birds especially. Time passed without his having any awareness of it as he gazed at the pretty creatures in the aviary, the little tiny red birds whose heartbeat could be seen through the feathers, the great-beaked parakeets, the glossy pheasants with silvery tails ...

Pat and Jack, meanwhile, with help from Sandie, had spread the picnic on a grassy bank in the sun. Sandie was enjoying herself thoroughly unpacking the goodies she had helped to prepare and those supplied by Mrs Sugden. Home-made scones with plentiful jam and butter, rich fruit cake in thick slices, little jellies in cardboard cartons with fruit gleaming in the yellow depths. 'No goodies until you've eaten up your sandwiches,' she cried, and offered egg-and-tomato or corned beef. To drink there was cider or coffee from the vacuum flask.

'I wonder what it's like to live in a place like this?' Pat remarked, thinking of the cleaning and housekeeping.

'Better than our caravan,' Sandie said round a mouthful of corned beef.

'You'd get lost trying to find your bedroom at night,' Jack suggested.

'Couldn't get lost at our place, that's certain. Although I've often thought that if we didn't have the footpath and had to go round the lane and then over the field, you could miss your way outside on a cloudy night.'

'Not if you take a torch,' Pat said in her practical fashion.

'Oh, *Mum*!' sighed Sandie, hearing her little drama thus done away with. She blew her dark straight fringe out of her eyes and examined the contents of the next polythene bag. Laughing, Pat brushed it back.

'Have to trim that for you, love. You'll be like an English sheepdog soon, lost behind the hair.'

'Woof, woof,' Jack said, offering Sandie a scone.

For some reason it was exquisitely funny. Perhaps it

27

was merely to do with being away from the confines of the caravan, without the glooming presence of her brother, out in the sunshine with two kindly grown-ups. Sandie laughed until the tears came to her eyes. She blinked them away.

Why couldn't her own father be like this, she asked herself.

Eventually Jackie found them and demanded food. He said little while he ate, but that little was at least amiable. He had a good tuck-in, said the fruit cake was great, and made no objection when Jack proposed they should put the picnic gear back in the car and then go for a walk round the grounds.

'Might see a deer,' he suggested. He sounded quite keen. His mother glanced at him in surprise but said nothing.

As the early November darkness began to fall they were heading back to Beckindale. 'I tell you what,' Jack remarked. 'Save you having to get a meal when you get back, how'd it be to come home to Emmerdale with me and take pot luck?'

'Oh, we couldn't impose –'

'Nonsense, Pat, Ma always has plenty in the larder.' If the truth were told, he'd already murmured to Annie that he might be bringing the Merricks back with him. Annie had at once told him it would be no problem but Jack's grandfather, overhearing, had scowled angrily and breathed some comment about 'that lot and their troubles.' Annie, casting a look at her father that had some reproof, had insisted it would be quite all right.

There was the usual cross-argument in the car about whether the arrangement would suit everybody. Sandie was quite keen; she had done all her weekend homework and rather wanted to see the inside of Emmerdale Farm. Jackie made grumbling noises at first but somehow it came into the conversation that Mrs Sugden kept geese, and he withdrew opposition although he didn't actually say he'd love to go.

Annie made no special fuss of them when they appeared. The kitchen was warm and welcoming in

28

contrast to the frosty nip of the evening. Hot tea was immediately forthcoming, and then a ham quiche warm from the oven, big wedges served with a salad, and lots of little cakes with different coloured icing on top. Sam, determined to be cool to them, found himself launched into reminiscences of his work with a former sheepdog, Diamond, known as Di. He liked the lass – a right smart little thing, catching on to everything he said. The boy had less to say for himself, but happen that was shyness, not sullenness. He came to life a little when Annie suggested she should take him to look at the geese.

'But we won't be able to see 'em in the dark –'

'Oh, I'll take the hurricane lamp. They'll come up to you, put their beaks in your hand.'

'Will they?' he said, eager despite himself.

'Want to try? Come along, then.' She put on a coat but didn't bother with wellingtons since the ground was already hardened with frost. She led the boy out of the warm kitchen and across the yard, round the corner of the mistle where the scent of disinfectant lingered in the air after the four o'clock cleaning. The pool of light from the lamp moved a little ahead of them. They came to the pasture where the geese were roosting, standing quiet, some with their heads under their wings. At the sound of her step and her voice, they roused themselves and came towards her, chattering in welcome and surprise.

She had brought a little grain to reward them for being disturbed. She gave it to Jackie. 'Throw some, and hold the rest.' He obeyed. The herd bent their heads to peck, but the old gander came up and put his beak in Jackie's half-closed fingers. It felt strange – dry, warm, alive. He could feel the soft feathers of the forehead against the side of his fist, make out the white back and the great, spread feet. 'Oh ... It's ... great,' he breathed.

Annie stood beside him in silence. She felt strange. Was it really true that this tall, inarticulate lad was her grandson?

Chapter Three

Towards the end of November a great event was to take place in Beckindale. This was the annual dance organised by the Allotments Association to raise funds for the expenses of running the association and staging the spring and late summer shows. This year it was to be made special by the addition of a fireworks display, held over from Guy Fawkes Day because the recreation ground, generally in use for that celebration, had been under repair until the end of the first week of November.

Jack, encouraged by the success of the outing to Harewood House, invited Pat Merrick to the dance.

'Oh, that does sound nice. Thank you, Jack.'

'You'll come, then?'

'I'd love to.'

He had met her toiling along the footpath with a laden shopping bag. 'I'll take that, shall I?' He relieved her of it and fell into step. 'I dropped in last night.'

'Aye, Sandie said.'

'She said you were working?'

'Late shift. Comes round every third week. We stay open till eleven, you know – catch quite a few of the long-distance lorry drivers cutting through to the motorway for an all night run.'

'That's awfully late, Pat. How d'you get home? There's no buses after nine.'

'No problem. Mrs Miles – the manageress, you know – she's always on and she gives late staff a lift home in her car. Means she doesn't get in herself till gone midnight but she doesn't seem to mind. She drops me at the lane end.'

'But you still have to walk to the caravan –'

'Not far, only ten minutes at most by the footpath.'

He was frowning as he stopped at her side while she

opened the door of the caravan. 'Couldn't you get something with easier hours, Pat?'

'Have to take what I can get.' She took the shopping bag from him and put it indoors. 'Thanks for the help.'

'Are you working tonight? Sandie said it was your day off.'

'That's right. I'll be working Saturday late turn this week.'

'How'd it be if I come for you – about half seven – and we'll go for a drink?'

'All right.' The words were cool but the tone was eager.

'See you then.' He paused as he was turning away. 'Kids all right?'

'Fine, thanks.'

'Sandie solved the mystery of the Star of Bethlehem yet?'

'She'd have told me if she had, I reckon.' She laughed. 'But Jackie still mentions the birds at Harewood from time to time.'

'That's good. Later, then. Bye.'

When they walked into the Woolpack bar that evening the landlord, Amos Brearly, nearly jumped out of his skin. He edged sharply up to his partner.

'Mr Wilks,' he hissed. 'It's Pat Merrick and Jack Sugden!'

'I can see it is, Amos,' said Henry.

'But I mean, it's the both of them.'

'Yes, Amos.'

'They came in together!'

'No law against it that I know of, lad.' Henry went to carry clean ashtrays to the far side of the room, putting an end to the exchange. All the same, he was as curious as Amos about the new arrivals.

Jack Sugden was something of a mystery to Henry. While it's a commonplace to say you can never really know anyone, he felt he knew Annie Sugden and her father and her son Joe as well as he could ever know another human being. But Jack was still something of a stranger to him.

31

Henry had read Jack's best-selling novel, *Field of Tares*. If, as all the critics had said, it was autobiographical, it told things about the author that Henry would never have let anyone know about himself. Yet that seemed to have been a different Jack Sugden from the man who now helped Matt Skilbeck to run Emmerdale. That Jack Sugden seemed to be conscientious, reliable, quiet-living, rather introspective.

But that quiet and conscientious man was apt to have fits of unexpected action. He had insisted on buying half a dozen pedigree cows to start Emmerdale on the road to a pedigree herd. It had been an almost spur of the moment decision, conceived and carried out within a few days. Henry found he was a bit suspicious of a man who could make such a decision, about so much money, with so little thought.

And yet, who could tell how long Jack had been thinking about it before he came out with it? Who could ever tell what he was thinking? Studying him now, laughing over some remark of Pat's, Henry would have said that here was a very ordinary man, out for an evening with an old friend. Amos, however, saw something deeper in it. And if you heeded what the whole of Beckindale was saying, and what that twerp of a reporter had published in his paper, Jack and Pat were old flames, former partners in a passionate affair.

Henry sighed and put the thoughts out of his mind. It was none of his business. Except ... Except that the estranged husband, Tom Merrick, had been seen around Beckindale looking like a thundercloud and, though Amos refused to listen to any mention of the Maltshovel, it was known that Tom Merrick went there fairly regularly to get drunk.

What was the meaning of this evening in the Woolpack bar? Henry could see other heads turning now and again towards the pair, could imagine the nudges between one man and the next. Jack must have known it would cause talk.

Was that why he had brought her here? Henry thought about that. If you wanted to let it be known that you were courting a girl, to take her out for an evening like this was just about the best way of doing it. Was this a declaration?

Could be. But, on the other hand, such was the coolness and detachment that Jack sometimes displayed, it might well be mere carelessness.

One thing was sure. If it got to the ears of Tom Merrick, it might cause trouble. Merrick had come ranting to Beckindale just after the feature article in the Sunday paper which more or less stated that Pat and Jack were about to resume a torrid affair. Only quick thinking by Annie and the local constable had averted a nasty scene.

If Merrick got to hear of it . . . and he would get to hear of it . . . Jack might be laying himself open to some unpleasant retaliation for befriending Pat. Extraordinary, sighed Henry to himself. The feller wouldn't let Pat have any kind of a decent life with him, and was bound and determined she wouldn't have it without him. A right dog in the manger – and a mean, vicious dog at that.

The news about Jack's evening out came to Joe when he started work next morning. Daniel Boxall, chief cowman, had been in the Woolpack the previous evening, later than Pat and Jack but while the bar was still buzzing with speculation. 'Mr. Anstey going to do owt about planting extra feed over winter?' Boxall began.

Joe was surprised. The plan for sowing feed crops had been discussed and settled in August. 'No, if there's a go-slow at Tomlinson's it'll happen soon. No point in planting extra for next year. Why d'you ask?'

'Thought he might plough up Lower Puddle Meadow.'

'What? Couldn't do that. Footpath runs across it.'

'Not used much, except by Pat Merrick and her young 'uns.'

'Well, it is used – and it'd be right awkward for Pat if she had to go the long way round.'

'Thought that prob'ly didn't matter now.'

'Didn't matter?' Joe said, staring at him with brown eyes which showed utter ignorance of the drift of the conversation. 'Of course it matters. So long as she lives in that 'van, she's got to have the use of the path.'

'Thought she was prob'ly gettin' wed.'

Joe was about to ask 'Who to?' but checked himself. Instinct told him he was being set up. He took a breath then said: 'That's bigamy, isn't it?'

'Bigamy?'

'She's already married. To Tom Merrick.'

'Oh, him. That's all over, I hear.'

'That so? Seems quick, if you're right. Divorce usually takes longer than that.'

'She got papers, I hear. Separated.'

'Oh aye, I know what you mean,' Joe said. 'Legal separation. That only means he's got to let her live apart, and stuff like that. They're still legally married, I think. Any road, she won't be marrying anybody else for a bit, so there's no problem about the footpath. Any case, Daniel – even if she did remarry, she might have her new husband living with her in the 'van.'

Daniel eyed him and began to talk about something else. His joke had sadly misfired. He intended to ask Joe if they were all invited to Jack's wedding to Pat Merrick, so as to act as a bodyguard against the vengeful Tom Merrick. But he was unable to resist a dig as they parted. 'Goin' to the Woolpack tonight?'

'Might do. Why, do I owe you a drink?'

'I expect you do, young Joe. Can't remember the last time you bought me one. Any road, it's an interesting place, the Woolpack. You see all kinds of interesting things there.'

Joe left him without further words. But he took the opportunity of a moment's respite to drive up to Emmerdale. There he heard the full story, such as it was. His grandfather was irate. 'Sitting there all evening with that woman,' Sam cried. 'Seth Armstrong were full of it!'

'Dad, what if he was?' Annie replied, casting a glance at Joe to ask for his help. 'Jack's got a perfect right to sit and drink with whoever he likes.'

'You know as well as I do, daughter,' Sam replied in a hard, indignant tone, 'that if he takes Pat Merrick to a place like that for everyone to see, it means something.'

34

He only ever addressed her as daughter when it was something very serious. Joe was startled to hear it.

'Now look here, Grandad,' he ventured, 'things are different nowadays. A feller can take a lass out for an evening without it being anything more than that – a few hours' companionship.'

'I should think he can find better companions than a woman who's left her legal spouse,' said Sam.

Joe had a hard job keeping his face straight. Legal spouse! Grandad really was in a stew, to be using phrases like that.

'There's nowt wrong wi' Pat Merrick,' he said. 'Except she's married to a waster.'

'Waster or not, it's her duty to stand by him. "For better, for worse" – that's in the marriage service.'

'That applies to him too, though, don't it, Dad?' Annie put in surprisingly. 'According to your way of looking at things, it's his duty to provide for her, care for her, defend her – is that right?'

'Well ... yes ... of course.'

'You reckon he's kept his side of the bargain?'

'Of course not, but it's her duty to try to bring him to better ways –'

'She's been trying for nigh on sixteen years, Dad. Wouldn't you say, if you'd been trying and failing for sixteen years, it's time to give it up?'

'I'm astonished at you, Annie. I never thought to hear you approving of a woman breaking up her marriage.'

'Pat didn't break it up. Tom Merrick did.'

'But it can be mended again if our Jack stays away from her.'

'Don't let me hear you speak like that to Jack,' his daughter warned. 'Jack's life is his own, and while he's living in this house no one is to tell him how to choose his friends.'

'Friends!' echoed Sam, shaking his head contemptuously. 'Is that what you think they are?'

'Dad!' cried Annie. 'Doesn't it say in the Catechism, "Keep my tongue from evil-speaking, lying, and slandering"?'

Sam sprang from his chair and stormed to the door. 'It's well said,' he remarked as he opened it, 'that even the devil can quote scripture when he needs to.' With that he stamped out.

'We-ell,' said Joe, sitting down. 'I hope he's calmed down afore he runs across our Jack.'

Annie sighed and busied herself making him some coffee. 'You know what he's like,' she said. 'He'll go off the boil by and by, but he'll never be able to resist getting in a dig or two whenever he can.'

'What's it all about, anyhow? Daniel Boxall was doing the minuet all round it this morning.'

His mother straightened her shoulders. 'I suppose the whole village is talking about it. I don't really know how much it means. It seems Jack took Pat to the Woolpack last night.'

'Big deal.'

'You can say that, but it causes talk.'

'Aye,' Joe agreed, 'there's no getting away from that. But did Jack realise that fact?'

'I don't know, and I'm certainly not going to ask him. And I hope no one else will, either.'

'I'll avoid the subject,' Joe promised. 'And if anybody starts on it with me, I'll squash it.'

'That's a good lad.'

But both of them knew that the action of Jack and Pat couldn't be cancelled out by not talking about it. What perplexed them was whether the consequences of the action had been realised by either of those two. Both of them had been away from Beckindale for a long time before returning to live there. Did they remember how traditional the society was? With younger people – a single man and a girl – it might have gone unremarked. But a man like Jack Sugden, with his terrible reputation as a Don Juan, and a married woman – Beckindale was bound to talk.

The expectation that something would come of it was justified. Two days later Tom Merrick showed up at the Woolpack.

Amos hadn't exactly barred him, but he'd always made

it clear he was unwelcome. That being so, Merrick generally went to the opposition when he was in Beckindale. Amos Brearly knew he was out for mischief the minute he came in. He edged along the bar to where Joe Sugden was deep in conversation with Richard Anstey over a midday drink.

'Joe ... er ... 'scuse me interrupting, but there's Tom Merrick.'

'Where?' Joe said, turning his head. Seeing him, he gave a nod of recognition and turned back to Anstey.

'Aren't you going to do anything?' Amos asked.

'What, for instance?'

Yes, what, for instance? Amos was brought up short. What could anyone do about Tom Merrick? You could hardly turn him out of the bar because he was a troublemaker, unkind to his wife, and bad news in general. And certainly Joe Sugden had no quarrel with him. Nor had Jack, if you came to think about it. Other way round, in fact. Tom Merrick might be said to have a quarrel with the man who was courting his wife.

If Jack Sugden was courting her.

Joe and Anstey resumed their conversation. The topic was Christmas trees. When Anstey said a few weeks ago that he would introduce Joe to the mysteries of forestry, it was Christmas trees he had in mind. After the first surprise, Joe had been quite intrigued. It seemed N.Y. Estates could make quite a lot of money out of Christmas trees.

'We'll just knock this back and then I'll give you a guided tour of the trees we're going to cull,' Anstey said. 'Won't take long and then you can go straight off to have your meal. Okay?'

'Ready when you are,' Joe said, draining his glass.

They got into Anstey's car and drove to the wood the far side of Ridge Farm. Joe had already seen the powerful machines at work there, handling huge logs onto a trailer where they were secured by thick strong chains for the journey to the sawmills. But they didn't stop there, they drove on to the plantation where the young Norway spruce stood in rows, between the larch trees.

'The larch is what we really get the money from,' Anstey explained. 'But as a catch crop Christmas trees don't do badly. Fifty pence a foot in the shops last year. I want you to take charge of the transport and extra labour. In about a week we'll start cutting, and as soon as they're cut they should be taken to market because the branches will suffer if they're on their sides too long. Right?'

'Right. How many men will I put onto it?'

'Three, I reckon – do you? Two to cut and stack, one to drive the truck. One load a day at about . . . say, three in the afternoon.'

'And they go where? Hotten?'

'Do you mind! Hotten! They go to a wholesaler in Leeds, who'll flog them plus twenty per cent to shops all round the area. Oh, it's quite lucrative, Joe. Short season but there's money to be made while it's on. Lasts from now till about a week into January – New Year parties like to have a tree on show and theatres running pantomimes generally have a tree in the foyer until mid-January.'

'Fancy that. I never knew all that.'

'Ah, stick with me, lad,' joked Anstey, 'and you'll get a thoroughgoing commercial education.'

'I believe you,' Joe said, and meant it.

The work on the Christmas trees was to start during the first week in December. That gave him time to sort out which of the men to put on the jobs. The Bonfire Dance was at the end of the week and with it came the end of November. Joe walked away, mentally choosing workmen.

Tom Merrick, certainly no workman, was still in the Woolpack. Amos was debating with himself whether to refuse to serve him if he asked for another drink. He'd certainly had enough.

'Same again,' Merrick said, putting his glass on the counter for a refill.

'Don't you think you should call it a day, Tom Merrick?'

'Eh? How d'you mean?' Merrick said, his cheeks above

the piratical black beard going red with annoyance. 'Only midday.'

'I mean you shouldn't drink any more. Not driving, are you?'

'Lost me licence, didn't I?'

'The bus for Hotten goes in a few minutes.'

'Nice of you to be so bothered for me, Amos. But I'm not going back to Hotten just at present. I've things to see to here. Aye,' he repeated, nodding sagely, 'things to see to.'

'Oh dear,' thought Amos, sensing bother. He meant trouble, did Tom Merrick, as surely as the sparks fly upwards.

Merrick drank up his last pint at leisure and took himself off. He was in no hurry. What he had to do would keep for a couple of hours. He found himself a snug corner in a barn on the N.Y. Estates and had a nap.

When he woke it was dark. He stretched and scratched and thought that a cup of tea would be nice. Well, where he was going, he'd hardly be refused.

His son and daughter were home from school, busy on their own activities. Jackie was reading *Melody Maker*, Sandie was hemming a dress for the school Christmas disco.

'Have you two listed who you're sending Christmas cards to?' their mother inquired, busy at the cooker.

'Yes, a long list of seven people!'

'You, Jackie?'

'What?'

'Know who you're sending cards to.'

'Oh, I'll think about it.'

'We need to know how many to buy, Jackie.'

'Why can't we buy a couple of them boxes of assorted? Seems quicker than choosing one by one.'

'Because it's more personal to choose each one –' She broke off as the caravan door opened and her husband walked in.

Sandie was first to recover. 'Hello, Dad,' she said in a very cool tone. Jackie gaped, Pat drew in her breath.

'Don't all look so pleased to see me,' said Merrick. Then, in a matey voice, 'Any chance of a cuppa?'

'It's just made,' said Sandie, and got up to fetch a cup and saucer. 'We were just going to have our meal.'

'Enough for a visitor, is there?'

Sandie turned a glance of appeal on her mother. It said, Don't have a row, Mum. After all, he is our Dad.

Suppressing a shudder of revulsion, Pat indicated the table. 'Take a chair,' she said. 'Fetch another plate, Sandie.'

The meal was sausages, eggs, and oven chips. Pat seldom had time to make proper meals except at the weekend, or her day off. But her husband showed every sign of enjoyment and wiped his plate with a piece of bread. 'That were grand, lass,' he said. 'Any more tea?'

'I'll make fresh, but we'll need more milk.' Pat nodded at Sandie and Jackie. 'You two, nip over to Home Farm and get some, will you?'

'Oh, Mum,' protested Jackie. 'Sandie can go on her own.'

'She's not walking about in the dark on her own, Jackie. Put your coat on and off with you.'

'But we can use powdered –'

'Come on, Jackie,' Sandie said with authority, and pulled at his arm. Her brother turned to look at her and she frowned at him. He understood that she was saying, Mum wanted to be alone with Dad. Sighing loudly, he pulled on his windcheater and went out with the pitcher for the milk, Sandie at his heels.

Tom had planned his campaign before he set off at mid-morning. Appeal to her sympathy, that was the way. 'I went after that job in Leeds,' he began, 'but it were gone afore I got there. The Job Centre sent me after summat at Connelton but they wanted a skilled carpenter. Think they might have taken me but another fellow came along, trained at Lowther's.'

'What a shame,' Pat said, but as if her heart wasn't in it. She had heard it all before, the excuses, the reasons that tried to cover up the fact that he'd never really tried. 'Well, perhaps you'll have better luck another time. Best

40

be going, hadn't you? If you miss the half-six bus there isn't another till nine.'

'I'd rather stop and talk to you, Pat. Look, I wanted to say, I got the message, so why don't you pack it in?'

'Message? What message?'

'Walking out on me, taking the kids with you. I know, I were a disappointment to you, hard to live with, I s'pose. But I've learned my lesson. Don't keep on with it.'

'Keep on?'

'It's time to come home. You're only making all of us miserable by carrying on like this.'

'Me making us miserable?' she cried. 'You've got a nerve –'

'I know, I know. I've been in the wrong, I don't deny it. But enough's enough. Get your cases out and come home.'

'This is home, Tom.'

'This little tea-chest of a place? Don't be daft! You can't stay on here –'

'I'm certainly not going anywhere else!' She sprang up from her chair and began collecting up the dishes with unnecessary vigour. 'Can't you get it through your head, Tom? We're finished, ended, all washed up. We're legally separated –'

'That? That's just a piece of paper –'

'It's a legal document and it means we're not to live together and the children are in my care. You've no right coming here trying to –'

'All I'm trying to do is get my family back. They're my kids as well as yours, you know.'

'Bit late to be telling me that, isn't it? If you'd helped me take care of them or earned a living for them, I'd have believed you meant it.'

'I mean it now, Pat. I've learned my lesson, I tell you.'

'Oh yes, until the next time. I've heard that kind of thing before too – and had the bruises to show how little you understood your own role as a husband.'

'Oh, we're back at that, are we? I'm uncouth and uneducated, is that it? Not good enough for you.' Despite

41

his intentions, his temper slipped. 'You always were a stuck-up bitch.'

She put her tray of dishes on the draining board and leaned there, turned away from him in aversion. 'Please, Tom. Just go.'

'Not afore I've said my say! If I haven't been able to get jobs, whose fault is that, eh?'

She turned, amazed. 'You're not saying it's mine?'

'Of course it's yours. Who used to press my suit and send me out after things I'd no qualifications for? Who got me laughed at for making applications I'd no chance of winning? Eh? Eh? And then you'd tell me it were my fault when I was turned down. Didn't really want it in the first place, you said.'

'Well, that was true enough, in all conscience.'

'And now you're turning the kids against me. Sandie's getting to be as stuck up as you are, and anybody can see Jackie isn't happy slogging on at school when he could get a job.'

'A job? Where is he going to get a job, with no qualifications?'

'Not around here, that's sure,' flashed Merrick. 'Chances are better for him in Hotten, and you know it.'

This had enough truth in it to silence her for the moment. He came to her, took her by the elbow, quite gently. 'Come on, lass, be reasonable. For the kids' sake, if not for ours – come back home.'

'It's for their sake I left,' she insisted, pulling away from him. 'Do you think it was good for them, seeing us constantly rowing?'

'And do you think it's good for them, you living here and being talked about all round the Dales?'

'I'm not being talked about –'

'Oh no? And that piece in the *Sunday Gazette* – that were all my imagination, then?'

'You know it wasn't. You gave that reporter an interview yourself, Tom!' she stared at him in perplexed anger. 'If I'm being talked about it's your fault.'

'Of course – everything's my fault, isn't it! But let me

42

tell you this, Mrs High-and-Mighty. If I catch you with Jack Sugden, you'd better watch out.'

'I'll be friends with who I please, Tom, and you can think what you like about it.'

'I'm thinking something I don't like–'

'And that's typical,' she flared. 'Always think the worst. Jack Sugden's only shown me a bit of friendship, that's all.'

'That'd better be all,' Merrick growled. 'Stay away from him.'

'Mind your own business!'

For a moment his arm came up, fist curled, as if he might hit her. Then he turned and flung himself towards the door. 'I'm warning you,' he said. 'Keep away from him. Don't think I won't know about it if you see him.'

He was gone, slamming the door behind him. Pat sank down on a chair. She had refused to let herself be browbeaten but she was trembling now.

She would have to tell Jack that she wouldn't be able to go to the Bonfire Dance. It was safer not to. She wouldn't tell him the reason because that would only make him stubborn.

So when she tried to get out of the engagement she failed. Jack couldn't understand why she was being so killjoy about a simple little country hop and a few fireworks round a bonfire.

'You were looking forward to it,' he pointed out. 'And don't tell me you have to work because I checked with Mrs Miles and she said you'd booked the evening free ten days ago. What's wrong, lass? Got nothing nice to wear?'

'No, no, it's not that–'

'Then there's no problem.'

But there was a problem though he was unaware of it. As he walked Pat home after the Bonfire Dance, he had a watcher taking note of all that happened. In the bushes that bordered Lower Puddle Meadow, Tom Merrick was shadowing them.

Nothing much to see, really. Two people saying goodnight after a pleasant evening. A quick pressure of

43

the hands, a sisterly peck on the cheek, a promise to be in touch soon. That was all.

But it only added fuel to the fire of resentment burning in Merrick's heart.

Chapter Four

Joe got his tree-cutting gang together on N.Y. Estates the Monday after the Bonfire Dance as per schedule. One man cut with a chainsaw, one tied branches together against the tree with thick twine and laid them aside. At half past two the truck arrived, by three they had them loaded aboard, by four o'clock they were being taken into the wholesaler's warehouse. It was a neat operation.

After the first day's work, Joe dropped in at Emmerdale to have a meal and discuss Christmas plans with his family. Then there were Dolly's home-made costumes for the Nativity Play to admire. What with one thing and another it was about half-past nine when Joe took his leave. Jack walked out with him to take a last look at the new calf.

As they came out of the calf-house, they heard a chainsaw in action. 'What was that?' Jack said.

'What? Didn't hear anything.'

But the noise came again. They both recognised it. 'Got your crew working at night, then?' Jack teased.

'At overtime rates? You out of your mind?'

'Funny time of night to be using a saw, though.'

'Somebody collecting firewood?'

'Who's got firewood rights around here except you and us?'

'Oh, well, Dodman's Common's not so far off. Happen it's coming from there.'

'Could be. Night, then.'

'Night.'

But the sound didn't come from Dodman's Common. Next morning, as Joe was on his way in the Land-Rover to Holly Farm about some breakdown in the sterilising equipment, the radio on the dashboard buzzed at him. He picked up the transceiver. 'Joe Sugden here, over.'

'Mr Sugden, Albert Folder sent word back to say, could you come to Ridge New Copse right away, over?'

'What's the problem? I thought the schedule for cutting and loading the trees was thoroughly understood.'

'I don't know, Mr Sugden.' The girl who ran the estate switchboard was efficient but uninvolved. 'I'm just passing on Folder's message.'

'Understood, over.' Joe was still not exactly pleased with this new contraption which could summon him at any time. All the same, he thought he'd better pay heed to it. He changed his route and drove to Ridge New Copse.

Richard Anstey, who had heard the call on his own set, was already there. 'It's a mess,' he said as Joe got out to join him.

'What's happened?'

'See for yourself.'

They walked in among the larches. The little Norway spruce trees had been hit as if by a hurricane. More than a dozen were simply broken off roughly. Others were half-broken, lying drunkenly at angles. Badly sawn stumps stood like fractured bones in the gloom of the plantation.

'My God,' said Joe.

'How many gone, do you reckon?' Anstey said to Folder, who stood by hugging his camouflage jacket around him in the cold air.

'I reckon they got upwards of a score away,' he replied. His breath came out like dragon steam. 'And they've wrecked about two dozen.'

'That's what I heard last night!' Joe exclaimed, thumping his fist into the palm of his other hand. 'Around half-past nine.'

'You heard them? And did nothing about it?'

'How was I to know, Richard?' Joe said. 'I thought it was somebody cutting up some old trunk on Dodman's.'

'I could wring their necks! It's bad enough to be robbed

45

of twenty valuable trees, but to crash about ruining more than they took . . . !'

'Who the devil could it have been?'

'We'll probably never know,' Anstey said, looking furious. 'They're off and away to Manchester or Leeds with 'em by now. Probably got the cash in their pockets – and who's going to ask the source of a few Christmas trees when they offer 'em cheap.'

There was nothing to be done about it. Anstey reported it to the police but more for the sake of being able to put it into his monthly report to head office and account for the loss of the trees than from any hope of recovering the stolen property.

'We can ask around to see if anybody noticed a van,' said P.C. Edwards. 'They had to have transport. And we have an approximate idea of the time.'

'Most folk were indoors by then,' Joe said.

'Aye . . . But I've an idea or two. No more than that, but I think I'll follow them up, Joe.'

'Good luck, Ted.'

'And of course we'll be keeping an eye on the plantation for a bit.'

'Not likely to come back, though, are they?'

'I s'pose not, Mr Anstey, but you never know your luck.'

Pat Merrick, tidying up at the Market Cafe after the lunchtime rush, was horrified to see her husband swagger in. He threw himself into a chair and said to her, 'Cup of coffee and gateau, love.'

'It's self-service, Tom, you know that,' she hissed.

'Oh, you can get it for me, can't you? Here.' He held out a pound note.

'I don't want you coming here, Tom,' she said, bending her head over her work.

'Then the sooner you get me coffee the sooner I'll be gone, eh?'

With a stifled groan she took the note and went to the counter. Mrs Miles, who knew very well who the customer was, filled the order in stiff silence and handed it to her on a small tray with the change alongside. 'I hope there's not going to be raised voices,' she murmured.

'No, Mrs Miles, of course not.'

When she put the tray down in front of Merrick he leaned back, looking lordly. 'Keep the change.'

'Nay...'

'Don't take tips? You'll never have owt put by for a rainy day that way.'

Feeling the eye of the manageress upon her and knowing it would only cause a wrangle if she refused, she took the elevenpence change from the tray. 'Good girl. I just dropped in to say ... Sorry about the other night. I shouldn't have said those things to you.'

'Forget it.'

'I can't forget it. I want us to get together again, Pat.'

'We can't discuss it here, Tom. You'll lose me my job!'

'Then you'd have to come back to me, wouldn't you – for support.'

She checked a bitter laugh. 'Not that I would – but when did you ever support us?'

'I told you before – I've turned over a new leaf, learned my lesson. I've got a little job now – only temporary but it pays well and the Social Security folk don't know so they can't dock it off my allowance –'

'Oh Tom! That's not the way ...'

'Don't be daft! Think I'm the only one who diddles them?'

'We don't want that kind of money –'

'Oh, so you've got all you want, have you? So you say! But what about the kids? They getting everything they want, wi' Christmas coming on?'

'We've enough, we don't expect to live in clover –'

'Oh aye, and what about Sandie? She's a young lady now, near enough. She getting nice shoes and hair clips like her pals?'

Pat thought about the party dress for the school disco, and couldn't respond that her daughter lacked nothing. The dress would turn out well – she and Sandie were good needlewomen. But the material was cheap and the shoes

47

and little handbag Sandie would wear with it were cheap too, and old.

'See?' Tom said in triumph. He took out two ten pound notes and let them flutter to the table. 'There you are.'

'We don't want it, Tom!'

'Next time I see the kids I'll ask 'em if they've got all they want and if they could've used a tenner each.' He paused, took a big gulp of coffee, and added, 'From their own father, too.'

'Mrs Merrick?' called the manageress.

Pat picked up the money. 'Please go,' she said. 'I'm supposed to be working, not chatting.'

'Right you are.' He picked up the gateau as he stood, bit a huge section and swallowed it, wiped his mouth with the back of his hand, and walked out. Charming, thought Mrs Miles to herself. The men some women got saddled with . . . !

As Pat walked towards the school later that afternoon, she was hailed by a well-known voice. 'Hello there, I looked in at the cafe but they said you were early turn this week.'

'Aye, thank goodness. What you doing here, Jack?'

'Collecting our new Land-Rover, that's what.'

'Oh, I thought there was a long waiting list . . . ?'

'Joe did a bit of a wangle for us so we could buy it through N.Y. Estates.'

'So N.Y. Estates have their good points, eh?' she laughed.

'Oh, nobody's all bad that can rent you a place to live, Pat.'

She hesitated. 'Tom has just been to the cafe –'

'More trouble?' he said quickly.

'Nay . . . In fact, it was sort of good news. He's got some kind of job.'

Jack's thin dark face showed a flash of disbelief which he quickly masked with an interested smile. 'Doing what, then?'

'He didn't say. But he's certainly flush with money. He gave me this for the children.' She took her hand out of her pocket, showing the two ten pound notes folded into each other.

'Ohh . . . ' murmured Jack. To tell the truth, he'd have been hard put to it to give away two tenners. 'That was generous of him.'

'Well, he's never mean with money when he has it,' Pat said, determined to be fair. 'It's just that he doesn't put himself out much to earn it as a rule.'

'Well, I'm glad he's got something. Lot of part-time work about, wi' Christmas coming on.' He gave a bit of a bow and a gesture of invitation. 'Can I offer to chauffeur you home in our new chariot?'

'Oh, that is kind of you, love. But no thanks, I'm meeting Jack and Sandie and we're going to choose Christmas cards afore we go home.'

'I see. Righto then. See you soon, Pat.'

She nodded and walked on. Tom Merrick, who had been tailing her from across the street some yards back, debated whether to catch up with her now as he'd intended or to let be. He'd wanted to follow up his advantage over being generous with the money and show off a bit to the kids. But if she'd arranged to meet Jack Sugden by and by . . . It'd be better to wait and see what happened, and maybe saunter up to them and make them feel guilty.

The whole plan misfired when his wife met no one but their children and went into a posh bookshop to linger over the trays of Christmas cards. Bored and annoyed, Tom packed it in and went into the Horse and Wagon as soon as it opened.

There he found his pal Derek Warne ordering a double whisky. 'Hey-up, Derek, don't flash your money about like that. That's a quick way to get the cops interested.'

'Oh, shove it. What's the good o' having money if you can't enjoy it? Sides, I can always say my auntie sent it to me for Christmas.'

'Who's your auntie supposed to be, then? Mrs Paul Getty?' Nevertheless Merrick also ordered a double whisky and sampled it loudly before getting down to business. 'We going to do them again, then?'

'Might as well. They're just sitting there, waiting to be cut, aren't they?'

'Not the same place, though. They'll be keeping an eye.'

'So they will, for a day or two. But Mr Plod hasn't got the man-power to be everywhere at once. So seems to me if we leave it a couple of days and then go to the other side of the plantation where they wouldn't be expecting us, it'll be a snip.'

'A snip!' laughed Merrick, taken with the aptness of the word for the cutting of Christmas trees. 'Snip, snip!'

Delighted with each other, they drank their whiskies. The barman eyed them from behind his newspaper and reckoned they were up to something, all flush with cash and drinking doubles. Local C.I.D. had dropped a word in his ear yesterday about tipping the wink over anyone with unexpected funds. He wouldn't put himself out, but if Sergeant MacArthur happened in, he wouldn't deny he'd seen something that might help.

After thinking things over, Pat Merrick decided that she must tell the children about the money their father had provided and use it for something they needed. The choice was easily made. She put it towards new shoes for Sandie and fashion boots for Jackie. Sandie was particularly delighted at being able to choose shoes that would go well with the new dress.

But Pat was still worried about the school disco. 'Oh, Mum,' sighed Sandie in the long-suffering tone appropriate to the anxieties of a parent, 'there's nothing to be in a tizz about. We'll get the last bus home and be here by ten.'

'That's what you say now. But you'll forget the time and be late for the bus –'

'No I won't, promise!' She nudged her brother. 'We'll be on time, won't we, Jackie.'

'Course we will.'

'I wouldn't mind so much if the Longthorns were picking you up as promised.'

'Well, they can't. They have to be in Scarborough that night. Some posh do.'

'We don't need the Longthorns,' said Jackie, who found young Andy Longthorn a drip. 'We'll catch the bus.'

'I don't like to think of you hanging about at the bus stop in the dark . . . '

'Oh, *Mum* . . . '

So it went on, until the problem was solved for them by the unlikely intervention of Joe Sugden. Jackie, having struck up a sort of friendship with the gamekeeper of N.Y. Estates, had asked if he could bring his mother and sister to see the pheasant hens in their coops sheltered by the Swinney covert. They were strolling back down the lane to the crossroads when Joe came by on an inspection round.

'Hello there! What're you up to, eh? Pinching sprigs of holly for Christmas?'

Pat laughed, Sandie smiled, and Jackie looked embarrassed. Seth Armstrong said: 'Don't mind, do you, Joe? I were just showing 'em the way we feed the hens until time for nesting.'

'Oh aye. Interested, are you, Jackie?' He'd heard from his mother about Jackie's delight with the Emmerdale geese. He fell into conversation with the boy about the problems of pheasant-rearing, and somehow into the general conversation there came a mention of the transport problem for the disco dance.

'I can solve that for you, easy,' Joe declared. 'I've got to be in Hotten that night for a session with N.Y.'s solicitor over leases for new tenants. How about if I pick you up after the dance?'

'But that'll be very late for you, Joe?' Pat said with hesitation.

'Not a bit. I'll finish with Collerby about eight-thirty, go and have a slap-up meal at the Red Lion, and be ready with my pumpkin and white mice to take Cinderella home. Okay?'

After some necessary discussion and gratitude, it was all arranged. Every cloud was banished from Sandie Merrick's horizon; she had a new dress, new shoes, would

51

dance with Andy Longthorn, and have a carriage awaiting when she was ready to go home.

That evening even Jackie enjoyed himself. The records played for dancing at the school disco were mostly by groups he admired and Sandie had stayed out of his hair. When they went out to the car park to find Joe, he was in a good enough mood to tell his sister that the whole affair had been 'not bad'. Joe Sugden was likewise pleased with life: Collerby had been brisk and easy to handle, the new leases looked like presenting no problems, and he'd had a sole bonne femme at the Red Lion with a half bottle of Piesporter.

They were driving down the dark lane that made a short cut between the Hotten road and Burnt Cross when Joe slowed suddenly. 'What was that?'

'What?'

'Thought I saw a light in the plantation.' He slowed further, stopped, half-opened the driving door and leaned out. No light. 'Must be seeing things,' he muttered.

But then, distinct on the still night air, came the buzz of a chainsaw.

'By heck!' he exclaimed. 'The cheeky tykes –' He slammed the door shut and drove off again at speed in the direction of the light he'd seen.

In the spruce plantation, Derek Warne watched a small Christmas tree topple sideways at the final touch of his saw, lit by the powerful battery lamp Tom Merrick was holding.

'That's enough, Der,' Merrick said. 'We've got sixteen aboard already.'

'Make it an even dozen and a half,' Derek Warne suggested with a laugh. He was applying the blade of the saw to the tree trunk when they both heard the sound of Joe's car engine approaching.

'Christ!' roared Merrick. 'It's the law!'

'Let's get out of here.' They threw the saw and the cut tree into the back of the van standing nearby with doors open. They clashed the doors shut, ran to the front and fell in. Warne was in the driving seat. He switched on and

52

pulled the starter but the van, on a carpet of spruce needles, wouldn't move at first as the wheels spun.

'Get a move on!' begged Merrick. 'They'll have us!'

Joe had swerved to a stop at the end of the avenue of trees. He got out, calling to the youngsters, 'Stay there!' He ran towards the indistinct outline of the van among the saplings. Next moment the van's motor was racing although no headlights came on. It bucketed about for a moment on the spruce needles then began to move forward.

'Mind what you're doing!' shouted Merrick, staring in horror as Joe's shape became clear in the light of his own car's beams.

'Mind yourself!' replied Warne, and seemed to aim the van straight at the running figure.

In Joe's car, Sandie screamed 'No!' Her brother, with some idea of protecting her from the sight, seized her by the shoulders and turned her away. At that moment the hurtling van veered to the side to avoid Joe's car. It hit Joe as he leapt out of its way, sent him sprawling among the trees.

As the van crossed the beam of Joe's headlights it lit up the faces of those aboard. Sandie, her head turned that way by her brother's protective arm, saw them clearly.

One was her father.

Chapter Five

The next few moments were a frightening blur. The van careered off into the darkness, still without lights. Jackie jumped out and ran to Joe, expecting to find him a mass of broken bones. Instead he found him trying to sit up, swearing horribly to himself.

'You all right?' he gasped.

'Except from having my teeth jarred into the back of my neck and every joint dislocated, I'm all right.' He clutched at his elbows, shrugged his shoulders, then attempted to stand. 'Help me up.'

Jackie did so. 'Come on, give me a hand back to the car.'

'You fit to drive?'

'No, but I'm going to – to the nearest phone to get the police.'

Anxious and upset, Jackie helped him into the car. Sandie shrank back in her seat, saying nothing. Jackie sat beside Joe as he drove gingerly to the telephone box at Burnt Crossroads. His first call was to Constable Edwards, his second to Richard Anstey, and then he rang Jack. 'Come and fetch these kids, Jack. We've had a bit of an upset on the way home.'

'Are they hurt?' Jack said in immediate anxiety.

'Them? No, they're fine. It's me that's been in the wars. Come on, big brother, come and get them. I don't feel up to it.'

Joe didn't feel much better next morning. He was a mass of bruises and aches. He had given the police all the information he could during the brief interview the previous night but now had to go to Hotten to make a statement.

'Want the two kids I had with me to make a statement?'

'Did they see owt?'

'Don't think so.'

'Then it'd only be unnecessary paperwork. Right you are then. Leave it with us, Mr Sugden. I think we may be able to put a finger on them now, what with your description of the van and probable damage to it –'

'I was more damaged than the van,' Joe groused.

'All t'same, the paintwork will probably show signs. Besides, we've got a bit of a lead already. We'll be in touch.'

This being so, Joe was inclined to make as little of the event as he could, so as not to alarm his mother. She had enough to be concerned about as it was, for the specialist in the orthopaedics department at the hospital, after looking at the X-rays, had diagnosed arthritic degeneration of the knee joint and decreed a replacement joint. When there was a vacancy in the operating list, Annie would be called for the operation.

'So just tell her I was in a bit of a brush with the Christmas tree rustlers,' Joe told Matt and Jack. 'As things turned out, I'm not much hurt.'

'Could have been nasty, though.'

'So it could.'

That was Jackie Merrick's view too. To him it had all been a great drama, a suitable ending to a good night out. He couldn't understand why his sister was so reluctant to talk about it next morning.

The day being Saturday, and Pat being on late shift at the cafe, she didn't have to go out early the next morning. She listened to Jackie's vivid description of the events, and noted Sandie's reticence. When Jackie had gone to the village to collect his copy of the *Melody Maker*, she made an extra cup of coffee for herself and Sandie then said, 'Come on love. Tell me what's wrong.'

'What d'you mean? I'm only a bit shaken up at what nearly happened.'

'It's more than that. You can scarcely bring yourself to speak about it whereas Jackie's full of it. What's the matter?'

'Nowt, I tell you.'

'It's no good trying to lie to me, Sandie. You never can bring it off.'

Sandie bit her lip. Tears brimmed in her eyes. She brushed them impatiently away. 'All right, if you must know – but you won't be happy when you hear it!' She broke off, then resumed in a stiff voice. 'I think it were Dad in that van.'

'What?' Whatever Pat had been expecting, it wasn't that. 'Trying to kill Joe Sugden by running him down?'

'Nay, that were another man – I don't know who that was. Dad were in t'passenger seat.'

'Oh, Sandie.' A little silence fell.

'I told you you were better not knowing.'

'Aye, lass. But whether I knew it or not, it's a fact.'

'I'm not *sure*, Mum. I just think it were him.'

'You know your own father, Sandie.'

'Aye.'

They sipped the instant coffee. Then Pat said: 'Seems like they don't want any evidence from you – the police, I mean. They seem to be happy wi' what Joe told them.'

'Thank goodness. I don't know that I could have told them what I've just told you, Mum.'

Poor little girl, thought Pat with compassion. She was only fourteen, after all. A rotten age to be, with all the pressures of coming womanhood. And to have to acknowledge the fact that her own father was a criminal . . .

'I think they're going to catch him, Mum,' Sandie said. 'The way Constable Edwards spoke last night – he seemed to think he knew where to go to find that van.'

There seemed nothing more to say. When Jackie at last came back with his pop music paper, by unspoken agreement they didn't mention their conversation.

Pat had a date for a lunchtime drink with Jack in the Woolpack. When she got there she found the bar buzzing with gossip about last night's drama but wasn't expected to play any part. Jack greeted her warmly and went to fetch the vodka and orange she enjoyed when she could afford it. He was full of concern about how the pleasure of the disco had been ruined for the two kids, but she told him Jackie had quite enjoyed the fracas. 'I'm sorry if Joe were badly hurt, though. Sandie said he seemed all right.'

'Oh, he'll survive. Finds it hard to stand up or sit down, but otherwise he's not much damaged.'

'In that case, Jack . . . '

'What?'

'Since no harm came of it, happen he won't want to press charges?'

'You what?' Jack said, staring at her with a baffled look on his thin face.

'I mean, if Joe's not taking it too hard . . . Mebbe he'd just as soon forget it.'

'I don't know if that's how he feels, but I'm darned sure Anstey doesn't. Another seventeen trees gone and plenty

56

of damage to those that are left, not counting the wreckage where the van careered into the young larches on its way out. That's theft and malicious damage, I imagine. And the police aren't going to let Joe drop charges against a man who could easily have killed him.'

'No. I suppose not.'

He studied her, then put a hand over hers on the table. 'What's behind this, lass?'

With great reluctance, and slowly, she told him Sandie's story. Jack whistled under his breath.

'D'you think Joe saw him?' she ended.

'I think he'd've mentioned it if he had.'

'Well, then ... You see, if Joe were to decide not to pursue the matter ... ' She was flushed with embarrassment. 'I mean, I know he's wrong to be stealing trees and all that, but Tom never meant to run Joe down – he weren't driving.'

'No, I suppose not.'

'So could you ... '

'What?'

'Ask Joe?'

'Ask him not to prosecute?' He shook his head. 'I don't think he'd take kindly to that.'

'How could Tom have been so daft!' she cried, then stopped short as heads turned her way.

'Don't let it upset you, lass. It's not your fault and not your responsibility –'

'Nay, but the children – what's it going to do to them if their father is charged wi' that?'

'Sandie knows already.'

'But us knowing's one thing. Having everybody else know – being made a poppy-show ... '

'I'll speak to Joe,' Jack said. 'I don't promise anything, but I'll try.'

They finished their drinks then he walked her home. At the door of the caravan she leaned towards him raising her face, and he bent to kiss her. It was the first time he had done so since that time, many years ago, when they had been young sweethearts.

''Bye, love,' he said with assumed cheerfulness as he walked away.

''Bye, Jack.'

Jack took the first opportunity of speaking to Joe about the attack with the van. He knew he daren't leave it, for the police seemed certain they were going to catch the villains before many hours were past. Joe was at Demdyke when he found him late that afternoon, painfully changing into a good suit and tie for an evening event in Connelton. 'Gamekeepers' Fair coming up,' he said. 'Organisers want to arrange the programme so we're having a bit of a get-together to discuss it. Help me get into this jacket, will you?'

'Shoulders aching?' Jack inquired.

'Eeh-h, I feel as if I've been through a mangle.'

'What's the news on that? Cops got the baddies?'

'I think the phrase is, "An arrest is expected". I hope they lock him up and throw away the key.'

'The feller that knocked you down, you mean.'

'Aye, who else.'

'I was wondering ... You see, Joe ... It seems likely Tom Merrick was in that van.'

Joe swung round to stare at him, wrenched his shoulder, and exclaimed in pain. Then he said, 'I might have known. It's just the kind of thing he'd do.'

'No, listen, Joe, he were the passenger, not the driver.'

'And how do you know that, if I may ask?' Joe said in a crisp tone.

'His lass saw him — as the van drove past she saw him in your headlights.'

'What, Sandie? She never said.'

'What d'you expect, Joe? Her own father!'

'Oh,' said Joe. He began painstakingly to tie his tie. 'It's a right old mess, isn't it? She told you about it then.'

'She told Pat, and Pat told me. She was wondering ... You see, Merrick didn't actually mean you harm.'

'Oh no. Just to the extent of robbing my employers of two hundred pounds' worth of trees, wrecking six rows of larch, and half killing me.'

'It was the chap driving the van who was out to get you, Joe. Tom was only trying to get a bit of cash for Christmas – give his kids a few extras.'

His younger brother turned on him a look of incredulity. 'Who fed you that sob story?'

'I know Merrick turned up with some extra money for the kids –'

'Listen, Jack, Pete Carstairs over by Church Lane wants to give his kids extras at Christmas but I don't hear of him taking a chainsaw to other people's property or aiming a van at anybody.'

It was only too true. Jack looked down. 'It'll be so rotten for Pat if Tom gets had up for this,' he muttered.

'I see. Doesn't matter if your brother nearly gets splattered over the forest floor. Much more important that Pat should be kept from feeling unhappy about it.'

Jack flushed and looked up, eyes glinting. 'No need to take that tone about it. I –'

'What tone d'you expect me to take? By heaven, for once I believe Grandad's right. You really can't see straight when it comes to Pat Merrick.'

'Joe, don't start quoting Grandad at me. We might end up saying things we'll regret!'

'As far as I'm concerned, there's nothing more I want to say. And if you don't mind, I'm in a hurry – I've got an appointment.'

'Oh, pardon me for interrupting the big businessman over some trivial human problem –'

'Get lost, Jack,' Joe said tersely, and turned to examine the knot of his tie in the mirror over the mantelpiece. For a moment the two brothers viewed each other through the reflection. Then Jack turned on his heel and went out.

At about that moment, Sandie and Jackie Merrick had got home from school in the fast-gathering dusk. On the doorstep of the caravan they could just make out some packages. Sandie opened the door and switched on the light inside. The packages then revealed themselves to be Christmas presents tied with bright tinsel string.

They carried them inside. On the tags attached to them

was written in round, childish characters, 'To Sandie with love from her Dad', 'To Jackie, Christmas Greetings from Dad', and 'To my dear wife at Christmas'.

'Gee-whizz, where did he get the money for all that?' marvelled Jackie. 'That must be a good temping job he's got!'

'Yes, it must,' Sandie said in a stifled voice. She couldn't help wondering what her mother would say when she saw them. She might even throw them on the rubbish tip.

But Pat couldn't bring herself to do that. Although she was sure they were bought with money dishonestly come by, it meant too much distress and explanation to refuse them. She let the children take the presents with them to Auntie Elsie's, where they were to spend Christmas, and even took the package intended for herself. It proved to contain talcum powder and soap of a brand she liked very much. Only Sandie noticed that she didn't use it.

There was no problem getting Jackie to write his thank-you letters this year. He wrote a card to Auntie Elsie saying how much he'd enjoyed all the Christmas fare she'd provided, which was quite true though he'd have preferred to eat it somewhere else. He wrote to an aunt in Dorset with gratitude for a knitted sweater. And he wrote a long letter to his father thanking him for the smart leather jacket with double zips on the pockets and sleeve edges. 'Smashing, just what I'd have chosen myself and if I get a motorbike it'll be just right to wear with it.'

The letter lay unopened for two days at Tom Merrick's untidy flat in Hotten. He was with the police, 'helping them with their inquiries.'

During the first week of January the news filtered through and was then made official by the report in the *Courier*: Derek Warne and Tom Merrick had appeared before the magistrate on charges of theft, malicious damage, trespassing with intent to cause damage, driving without due care and attention, causing actual bodily harm, and defrauding a wholesaler. Both men had been released on bail on their own recognisance and were to appear at Hotten Crown Court during the coming sessions.

When the paper came out, Joe went in search of his brother. 'I didn't say owt about what you told me, Jack,' he said, uncertain how to put it. 'I mean, they were going to charge Merrick any road. They had plenty on him. I didn't say you knew he'd been in that van.'

'No, of course not, Joe.'

'I don't say I'm sorry for the bloke – he brings it all on himself, if you ask me. But I'm sorry I lost my temper with you that night.'

'Yeh. Me too.'

'How're the Merrick kids taking it?'

'Dunno, Joe.' He shrugged, shaking his head. 'I don't see as much of them as you seem to think.'

'No?'

'Look, I've known Pat a long time. You know that. D'you expect me to turn my back on her when she needs a friend?'

'It's your business, Jack, not mine. But I can tell you from bitter experience that it's an uphill task turning a deaf ear to the gossips in Beckindale, lad. They broke up me and Kathy in the end. Think on!'

'But they've nothing to gossip about! Pat and I –'

'Are just good friends, eh?' Then, seeing the rebuke forming on his brother's lips, 'Sorry, I didn't mean to be cheap about it. But that business with Hilleley and the *Sunday Gazette* should have taught you – nothing you do goes unobserved.'

Jack nodded and shrugged. They went on to talk of farming matters. Later he let his attention go back to Joe's words. "Nothing you do goes unobserved." In a small community like this, of course the actions of two people as intriguing as himself and Pat Merrick must cause talk. Jack was interesting because he had written a strange best-selling novel, had been a returned prodigal, was something of an unknown quantity with his new resolve to be a good farmer. His source of income caused speculation. He had enough money to buy pedigree cows and help finance a new long-base Land-Rover – how much, they no doubt wondered, did he have squirrelled away in his bank account? And how did he intend to use it? If he was so bothered about Pat Merrick, why didn't he give her money enough to tide her over this bad time?

Pat was interesting because in the past, long years ago, she had been Jack's girl. He had left the neighbourhood unexpectedly and with almost equal suddenness Pat had married Tom Merrick. The first child of their family, Jackie, had been, in the age-old term, "a seven months babe". It was easy to guess there had been a lot of talk about whether Pat and Tom had had to get married to give the expected child its father's name. Or, the gossips asked each other, had the child got another man's name? Was Jackie Merrick – significantly christened Jack – really the son of Jack Sugden?

Now she had left Tom Merrick. No one really thought the worse of her for that, because everyone knew Tom Merrick was a no-good. But now she and Jack Sugden were seen around together.

Of course it was going to cause talk, Jack realised. Perhaps he should stop seeing her. Yet she needed a friend. It would be cruel to turn his back on her. All kinds of emotions bound Jack to her, and important among them were guilt and pity. If he hadn't left Beckindale seventeen years ago, Pat would never have married Tom Merrick. He was to blame. He must try to make amends now. He must stand by her.

The same feeling of loyalty was evinced by the Merrick children, towards their father. 'We ought to go and see him, Mum,' Jackie said. 'Show we're standing by him.'

'Aye, we ought,' Sandie agreed.

Their mother was shaken at the intensity of their manner. 'I don't think you–'

'*You* don't need to come,' Jackie said with sullen resentment. 'We'll go on our own.'

'After school,' added Sandie.

'Aye.'

'You'll miss t'school bus–'

'We'll catch the ordinary bus.'

62

Pat sighed. 'Got money for the fare?'

'Dad'll give it us.'

Out of the money he earned from stealing Christmas trees, Pat was about to say. But she held her tongue. 'Here,' she said, opening her purse and taking out silver, 'you'd better have it in case.'

Jackie looked as if he would refuse it. Sandie took it and put it in the new little disco handbag her mother had given her for Christmas. Her brother flashed her a look that said, 'Traitor!' Stung, Sandie said, 'I'm giving up Debating Society meeting to come.'

'Oh, the sacrifices we make for family loyalty!' sneered Jackie. 'Fancy – giving up half an hour's dreary chat about "Should the voting age be lowered to seventeen?'' And all just to visit your own father.' He pushed away his breakfast plate. 'But at least you are coming.'

'I expect he's all right, really,' Sandie said with a nervous glance at her mother. To her, the matter wasn't so black and white as to Jackie. She had seen her father in the van that might have killed Joe Sugden.

'You can be sure he's all right,' Pat said, unable to stem the bitter words. 'He always manages to fall on his feet.'

'No thanks to you!' flashed Jackie. 'You were quick enough to get a lawyer to help when you wanted to get shot of him but I didn't see you rushing to him when Dad had to come up in court.'

'He had a lawyer allotted to him by Legal Aid –'

'It'd have looked a lot better if you'd done that for him, and turned up in court –'

'Why are you putting it on to me?' his mother cried, brushing her hair back from her flushed, tired face. 'I'm not responsible for the mess he's got himself into, nor any of the others that went before. I'm just the one he leaves to keep you fed and clothed while he gallivants off after easy money. I'm just the one who has to pretend nothing's happened when I get dirty looks and folk whispering after I've walked by. But do I get any help from you two?'

Jackie got up, almost pushing his chair over with the vehemence of the movement. 'It's Dad that needs the help,' he said. 'Come on, Sandie, we'll miss the bus.' He went out and stalked down the cinder path away from the caravan. He paid no heed when his mother called after him, 'Take your jacket, Jackie.'

Sandie stood up likewise and put Jackie's chair tidily against the table. She picked up her brother's jacket from the hook by the door. 'He doesn't mean to be rotten to you, Mum,' she muttered. 'He's upset.'

Pat sighed and nodded. 'It's easy to think I'm the only one wi' problems,' she agreed. 'Look, Sandie . . . did you ever mention to him about . . . you know . . . seeing your Dad that night?'

'Of course not.' The tone said, 'You don't tell important things like that to boys.'

'I don't know whether it's better he doesn't know, or not.'

'What difference does it make? Dad's going to get it in the neck and Jackie knows it. The worse the case looks against him, the more Jackie's going to stick up for him.'

'Aye . . . Well, don't stay too long with him this evening, love. Whatever Jackie may feel, the court awarded the two of you to my care and I don't know how it'd look to the social worker if she heard you were spending too much time with a man charged with serious offences.'

'Oh, him!' Sandie said. She resented Mr Instone, the social worker for the local council, whom she regarded as an interfering busybody despite his trendy appearance and his knowledge of current pop slang. 'Bye, Mum. See you.'

She went out winding a scarf round her neck and carrying Jackie's jerkin. He was standing at the edge of the footpath, looking frozen in the chill morning wind. She handed him his jacket. 'You are an idiot, Jackie!' she said offhandedly and walked past him, fed up with him, with life, and the world in general.

Jackie put on his jacket and ran with long easy strides to catch up with her. 'Sandie . . . D'you think it's right, the way she won't even come with us?'

'Right? What d'you mean, right?'

'Oh, come on, don't sound like the Debating Society. After all, they are married.'

'Separated.'

'That means nowt, really. Mr Instone said it was a temporary thing while they sorted out their problems.'

'They're never going to sort them out if they keep getting more of them all the time.' She was thinking of their father's undeniable propensity for getting into trouble.

'Aye,' agreed Jackie. He was thinking of Jack Sugden, about whom he'd had some teasing from his school friends.

And their mother, clearing up the breakfast things, was thinking about both those aspects, without much idea of the outcome.

Chapter Six

The short, dark days of January dragged on, bringing with them heavy snows and deep frosts. The cloud cover was so heavy that sometimes the only light seemed to be the reflection of the snowdrifts. The go-slow among the feed merchant's drivers turned into a strike. Only neighbourliness from N.Y. Estates in sharing their stored feed enabled the other farmers to keep their stock. 'Y'see, they're not all bad, after all,' Matt Skilbeck said to Jack and he, somewhat vexed, had to admit he was beholden to them yet again.

When the first snowdrops peeped through, with their message that the farming year was on the turn, problems were by no means over. It became urgent to decide what to do about the long-planned Farm Museum; Ed Hathersage needed to sell the land earmarked for the project so either Henry had to buy it and make the Museum work, or give up the idea. A visit to a county-council museum told Henry that the costs were beyond the income of any voluntary scheme. Sadly, he abandoned that dream. A period of uncertainty followed in which N.Y. Estates showed up in what Jack felt was their true colours, by trying to buy the Hathersage land from under the Emmerdale family's nose. It ended with Hathersage agreeing to rent the land to Emmerdale Farm Limited at a reasonable rate.

Joe had gone along with it very reluctantly. 'You're taking on too much,' he told Jack. 'You're never going to manage, just you and Matt. And getting that sour land into good heart is going to cost Emmerdale a fortune.'

'But it'll be worth it if we really go into beef production. You said so yourself.'

'I know I did. But that's for a company that can afford long-term investment, Jack. And wi' staff to handle the project.'

'We'll manage,' Jack said with stubborn determination.

But it left him no time for rallying round to help Pat Merrick – which was perhaps just as well, for Tom Merrick had taken to dropping in unexpectedly at the caravan.

When he was arrested and charged by the police, Merrick had been very downcast. He knew Pat would abhor what he had done. But to his own astonishment it seemed to call out a protective loyalty in the kids. It was they who came to him at first. Emboldened by that, he would come to the caravan when they were home from school but Pat was still at work. Sandie generally welcomed him then busied herself with her homework, but Jackie was always ready for a chat.

'You don't get much o' that, then?' Merrick said to Jackie, nodding at Sandie's exercise book and textbook.

'Yeah, supposed to do it, but what's the point? I get a copy from another feller in the morning.'

'Not much for schoolwork, then, lad?'

'Waste of time, isn't it? What's the point – fellers who left school with O and A levels – they've not managed to get jobs worth bragging about.'

'Not much in the way of jobs around here, in any case.'

'No, but if I lived in Hotten, it'd be different.' Jackie

66

began to gather enthusiasm, his voice becoming less of a moan. 'I'm good with my hands, Seth says so –'

'Seth?'

'Armstrong – lets me help making coops for his pheasants and that. You don't need certificates to do that. I reckon I could get a job, happen in painting and decorating, in Hotten.'

'It's a shame you can't live wi' Derek and me,' his father remarked in a tone of regret. 'Plenty of room there. Had to give up the flat, tha knows – couldn't afford it on Social Security. But we manage all right, me and Der.'

'Just the two of you?' Jackie said eagerly, envisioning a world in which females didn't nag at him to pick up his clothes, eat up his food, and turn down his radio.

'Aye, it's all right. Liberty Hall, it is.'

'It's his place, is it?'

'Aye, but he's easygoing, a good lad. You should meet him some time, Jackie. You shouldn't believe all you hear about him – he's all right.'

Sandie looked up at that point to remark that she had better get started on making the evening meal.

'Mum be home soon, then?' her father inquired.

'Five-thirty, thereabouts.'

'I'd best be off, then.' He gave them a conspiratorial smile that was tinged with sadness. 'Don't approve of me coming to see you, does she.'

'We won't tell her,' Jackie said.

'Good lad. Here, got any use for a bit o' cash?' He produced two fifty pence pieces and put one before each of them on the table.

'I thought you were having a hard time, on Social Security?' Sandie said, looking at the money.

Merrick gave a wink. 'Little job putting glass in a window, earned a couple of quid,' he said, taking them into his secret. 'Don't tell Mum that, either.'

'Sure you can spare it, Dad?' Jackie murmured, unwilling to leave him short of money but unwilling too to hurt his feelings by refusing.

'More where that came from,' Merrick said, taking his

leave. 'There's always little jobs for a fellow that's good with his hands.'

With that he left, knowing that Jackie would now be dreaming of all the little jobs he could do if only he were in Hotten with his Dad.

Annie Sugden had had a letter telling her there would be a bed for her in the local hospital in ten days' time. The operation suddenly loomed large and menacing over her. 'Do you think you'll be able to manage, love?' she asked Dolly Skilbeck as they talked it over. 'You know the routine by now, but having to do it all without help is a big thing.'

'Don't you worry about it, Ma,' Dolly soothed. 'You concentrate on having the op and getting it over with.'

'Aye, I'll be glad when it's done. It's been getting quite a nuisance, this knee.'

Dolly was well aware that the knee had been more than just a 'nuisance' for some months now. It had quite angered her that the menfolk seemed not to notice how often Annie was in pain. But she knew Annie didn't want a fuss made about it so she had held her peace. Now that the operation was to be done, Dolly was determined to run the house like clockwork so that Annie would have nothing to worry about.

Inexorably the days passed and Annie was driven to the hospital. Her father, left at home to help Matt, seemed almost in a dream at the idea of not having his daughter about the house as usual. Jack, who drove her into town, was white with unspoken anxiety, his long rectangular face set in determined calm. It was Annie herself who was the most normal of all of them. 'Don't worry, I'm in good hands,' she said at leave-taking. Jack thought she meant the surgeon. His grandfather could have told him she meant the Almighty.

She was right, of course. The operation was carried out the following day without difficulty or complication. The news, when they telephoned, was that she was well and coming out of the anaesthetic. Visitors would be permitted next day. Jack drove his grandfather to see her, bearing a huge bunch of chrysanthemums. They found her sitting up with a cage contraption over her legs and the bedside cabinet crowded with get-well cards.

'Eeh, lass,' Sam said, taking her hand.

'Now then, Dad,' she said gently.

With that calm exchange he told her he had been worried to death and she told him she was perfectly all right. Jack, watching them, thought that even when he had imagined himself to be writing scenes of great sensitivity in his novels, he had never approached the quiet but deep affection of those words.

Joe visited at the evening session. 'Best place to be,' he told his mother. 'It's bitter out.'

'It's too warm in here – look how the flowers are wilting.'

'I brought you grapes. You always have to bring grapes to folk in hospital.'

She laughed. 'And now you'll sit and eat them yourself, if I know you.'

Nothing could have reassured him more. She was making a perfect recovery from the operation. Now all that remained was for her to learn to walk on the repaired knee joint. That might take a few weeks but, so they all told him, she would be as good as new afterwards.

The following afternoon it was to be the turn of Matt and Dolly. Jack too was going, although only two visitors at a time were allowed. The plan was that Dolly and Matt should go first while Jack waited in the corridor. Dolly was packing a shopping basket with the various items she'd been asked to take: Annie's reading glasses, a copy of *Radio Times* so she would know what was on the radio earphones, a library book, and – though Dolly felt it was too early yet for her to feel strong enough to knit, a half-finished cardigan. Jack was to take a jigsaw puzzle from Henry and a bottle of stout donated by Amos, who said it was well known that stout was good for building up strength after illness. If Jack thought it very unlikely that his mother would ever drink stout, he kept the thought to himself.

They were all assembled and checking their packages

when the phone rang. 'Dratted thing!' exclaimed Sam in vexation. He had little time for the telephone and less still when it rang just as folk were going out on some important project.

Knowing it was no use expecting Grandad to pick up the receiver, Jack put down his burdens and answered the phone. To his astonishment, it was Pat Merrick. She had never rung him before.

'Can I speak to –? Oh! Is that you, Jack? Jack, something dreadful's happened! Jackie's run away!'

'You what?' exclaimed Jack.

'He's gone. Left a note to say he hates living in t'caravan and he's gone to Hotten.'

'But ... but ... where would he go?' He broke off. 'Oh, you mean –'

'I don't know where he's gone, Jack! I don't think he can have gone to his father because Tom's moved out of the flat a long while back. Jack, what am I going to do?'

'Have you contacted that chap –'

'The social worker? Nay, I want to keep him out of it. I thought of you, first off, Jack.'

'But I'm –' He was going to say, 'doing something important.' But after all, what was more important than the wellbeing of a teenage boy? 'I'll be right there, Pat.' He put the phone down, turning to avoid his grandfather's accusing eye. 'I have to go out,' he said to Matt. 'I'll follow on later. It fits any road – you were going to go into the ward first.'

'Aye, right you are,' Matt said, and taking Dolly by the arm, went out.

Jack looked for and found the keys of his mother's car. 'You're not going to the hospital then?' Sam inquired angrily.

'Not right away.'

He hurried out, only half-hearing Sam's last words. They sounded like: 'You'd put that woman first?'

When he reached the caravan he found Pat almost beside herself. She handed him a piece of paper as he came in. On it was written in Jackie's untidy scrawl: 'What's the point in going on at school when I could leave and get a job, so I'm going to find something to do in Hotten. Don't worry, I'll be all right, and anyhow you know I hate living here. Yours, Jackie.'

'Had you any idea this was coming?' Jack inquired, sitting down at the table.

'Not the least. Nor had Sandie, I'm sure. Sandie went off to school same as usual this morning. Jackie was a bit late so I left him looking for a schoolbook he said he needed. I was on nine-to-one shift today, my half-day off. He must have waited till I was gone, packed his things, and taken the ten o'clock bus to Hotten.'

'He must have gone to Tom,' Jack said. 'Where else would he go?'

'I suppose so. But how would he know where Tom's living? Someone who I used to live next door to, she told me he'd given up the flat. If Jackie's gone there, he'll find him gone.'

'Then he'll come home, surely.'

'I . . . suppose so.'

Jack thought for a moment. 'It seems to me . . . '

'What?'

'That Jackie's probably been seeing his father since the court case.'

'They went – they both went – just after the magistrate's court. They felt they ought to.'

'Solidarity,' Jack said with a wry smile.

'Something like that. But Sandie felt she'd done her duty, more or less. I think Jackie felt they ought both to have done more.'

'So . . . look here, Pat . . . if he's gone to Hotten he's gone to Tom. Either he doesn't know he's moved from the flat, in which case he'll find it empty and come home, or he knows where to find Tom.'

'In which case he won't come home,' Pat ended in a scared, weary tone.

'Not right away. But after all, happen he won't find it so much fun as he imagines. Doing your own cooking and laundry's no fun – I know, I did it for months after I first left home. And what will he do for money?'

'Tom always manages to have money, Jack.' She cast

her mind back. 'They both had some extra pocket money the other day. I couldn't quite understand it but thought mebbe it was Christmas money they'd put by. Now, I think probably Tom gave it to them.'

'So they have been seeing him.'

'Oh, what a mess!' she cried, walking about the confined space of the living room with her hands clenched. 'He knows the kids were put in my care as being a fit person. He knows he wasn't supposed to see them without my agreement.'

'If you report it to the social worker, he'll bring Jackie back straight away –'

'No! I don't want him dragged back. There's enough bad feeling between us –'

'Bad feeling? Between you and Jackie?' Jack was shocked at the words.

'You don't know what it's been like! Somehow he seems to think I'm to blame for what's happened to his Dad. It's no good me saying Tom's always been in trouble, he doesn't believe it. You see, I used to try to keep it from them when they were small. It's only recently our rows got to the stage where they couldn't be hidden – and Jackie's got the notion I'm as much to blame for that as his father.' She turned away, head bent. 'And happen he's right.'

'Nay, lass, don't take guilt on yourself that doesn't belong there. Tom Merrick was always a hard case.'

'But I knew that when I married him. I shouldn't have held it against him that he was what he was.'

The question hovered in the air between them: Why did you marry him then? But Jack didn't dare to ask it because he wasn't ready to hear the answer. And besides, this wasn't the time. He said: 'It comes down to this, then. It's fairly sure Jackie's gone to Tom. Do you want me to go and find him?'

She shook her head quickly. 'Nay! That would be too much of a defeat to him.'

'Leave him to come back in his own good time, then?'

'But suppose Mr Instone comes visiting?'

'You could say he was out with friends. Surely Jackie isn't always in when he calls?'

'I don't remember. Probably not!'

'That's it then. Give it a day or two?'

She was silent for a long moment. Then she said sadly, 'I suppose so. I'll tell Sandie not to say anything at school.'

'This isn't good for Sandie either,' Jack said with a sigh.

'It isn't good for anybody. I shouldn't have dragged you into it, Jack.'

'Rubbish. You can always call on me.' He turned to go. 'I'm visiting Ma in hospital but I'll be in touch when I get back. Okay?'

'Okay. And thanks – talking to you about it has cleared my mind.'

He nodded and went out. Only when she heard the car start up and drive off did she allow the tears to brim over in a hot, bitter tide.

Jackie didn't come home next day, nor yet the next. His younger sister couldn't help being quite pleased at the tranquillity that settled over her home now that he was away. If it wasn't that it made Mum look so tense and unhappy to have him gone, Sandie would have enjoyed the respite.

On the following day came the visit, half-expected, from Mr Instone. Jackie had not been to school and Pat had sent no note making excuses about it. Jackie's form master had mentioned it to the headmaster and the headmaster, well aware of the various troubles that beset the Merricks, told the social worker.

Yet Mr Instone wouldn't have put that up at the top of his list of priorities, which were many. Jackie Merrick was after all turned sixteen and fully entitled to stop attending school if he could persuade his parents on that point. That might be the explanation of his non-attendance. Although Pat had been apprehensively awaiting Instone's visit, his first words took her totally by surprise.

'I've persuaded the police not to take immediate action, Mrs Merrick. I said I could probably sort it out with you. But you've really got to keep a stricter eye on him.'

'What?' Pat said, backing away to let him come into the living room. 'Who – you mean Jackie?'

'He hasn't told you?'

'No – what?'

'He'll have to develop more of a sense of responsibility, Mrs Merrick. I'm ready to do my best for him, but he's got to play his part.'

'But what's he done?' begged Pat, with visions of mischief initiated by her husband, with Jackie tagging along.

'Well, inquiries are still going on but it seems to amount to taking away a motorcycle without the owner's consent, driving without a current licence, and not wearing a safety helmet.'

'Oh my God,' Pat said, and sank down on the nearest chair with her face so white that Instone thought she was going to faint.

'Mrs Merrick! Are you all right?'

'Yes, yes, I'm fine. I just . . . it was the surprise . . . '

'He hasn't told you?'

'When did all this happen?'

'Yesterday.'

'In Hotten?'

'Yes. And of course I know he hasn't been to school. What's he been doing – going into Hotten on the school bus and truanting?'

'Mr Instone, I'm sure our Jackie never stole a motorbike. He may be a bit difficult from time to time but Jackie's no thief.'

'I agree with you. His story is that Graham Jelks lent him the bike, so I hear. Does he know a Graham Jelks?'

'Yes, he does, they're great mates.'

'Oh then, it's probably true. That charge will be dropped. But he hasn't got a driving licence, has he?'

'Are you joking?' Pat said bitterly. 'We couldn't afford it, nor a bike for him to ride if he'd got a licence.'

'Right on. So he hasn't got a licence and he hasn't got a crash helmet.'

'No, he hasn't.'

'Listen, I can't stay, I've got other cases to look after

74

today. When he comes in, tell him you know all this and put a scare into him. He's got to behave himself because, if he doesn't, a care order might be made.'

'A care order? But he's in my care.'

'If you can't control him he may be deemed in need of proper care and taken into a council home. He doesn't want that, Mrs Merrick, neither do you, neither do I. Make him see sense, no jiving. It'd be better if he'd go back to school and better still if he'd enrol to take O levels. It's got a reassuring sound to local authority child-care departments, a lad taking O levels.'

'But will he be prosecuted about the bike?'

'If this lad Jelks really lent him the bike, the fuzz will probably let the rest slide. A lot of paperwork about nothing, you see. But they'll give him an earful, I've no doubt. And he'll deserve it. He's behaving like a half-wit.'

'I'll talk to him, Mr Instone,' she assured him. Refraining from adding, 'If I can find him.'

Jack Sugden had told her he was ready to help at any time. She rang him and asked if he could meet her in some quiet spot that evening. He arranged to call and take her to Connelton for a drink, knowing it must be something to do with either Jackie or Tom if she couldn't talk of it in front of Sandie.

Although it was hardly appropriate, the idea of going to Connelton seemed to make it a special occasion. Pat took special pains with her mane of thick brown hair, and put on her one good dress. Sandie, surveying her as she picked up her handbag to go out, said with unexpected warmth, 'You look a treat, Mum.'

'I don't know how! I feel awful.'

'I think you agonise too much over Jackie,' the girl said in a thoughtful tone. 'Happen if you just let him fall down and pick himself up, he'd do less stumbling.'

'I can't help it, love. If I don't worry about him, who will?'

Sandie hadn't heard the details of the visit by Mr Instone. But Pat had felt she had to say there was a bit of a problem about Jackie. Sandie understood quite well that this evening with Jack Sugden was to discuss what to do. 'Have a nice time – or at least as nice as possible,' she urged.

'Aye. Shan't be late, love.'

When she was in the Land-Rover beside Jack she explained the latest development. Jack groaned inwardly. He hadn't the least doubt that Jackie was with Tom Merrick. That being so, and considering that Jackie and Tom were supposed to be close, why couldn't Tom Merrick take decent care of the boy?

'You didn't tell Instone that Jackie wasn't living with you at present?'

She shook her head. 'He didn't ask, just took it for granted Jackie was out. He actually said summat about Jackie taking the school bus in each morning and then truanting. I didn't say he'd left home.'

'Mmm . . .' said Jack and gave it some thought.

They went to the Feathers in Connelton and ordered a bar-snack in the elegant 'snuggery' with its candle-lit alcoves and old barrels as tables. Pat would have sworn she had no appetite, but when food was placed before her – elegantly served food that she herself had not had to prepare – she found she was hungry. As they ate, they let the problem drop for the moment. Then Jack said: 'Best thing would be to get him home before Mr Instone comes again, and before the police catch on. It looks as if Jackie must have given the caravan as his address, doesn't it?'

'I suppose he must have.' She sighed. 'He's learning to be deceitful. He never used to be like that.'

'Don't start taking blame to yourself, lass. It's not your fault. It was Jackie's choice to go and live in Hotten, and it was his choice whether or not to tell the truth to the cops. He decided not to. It may turn out all right – if we can get him back.'

'It's no use me begging Tom to let him go,' she said. 'It'll only make him the more determined to keep the boy.'

'You want me to go and talk to him?'

'To Tom?'

'To Jackie. Somebody's got to.'

'Would you, Jack? He doesn't listen to me any more.'

'I'll do it if you want me to,' Jack said.

'When could you go?'

'Sooner the better, Pat. The longer we leave it, the more likely the police are to realise he lied to them. That won't look good. It'd be as well to go tonight.'

'Tonight?'

Jack looked at his watch. 'It's not nine o'clock yet. If I go straight from here, I can be in Hotten in fifteen minutes. I'll tell you what – you stop here – I'll get them to bring you a tray of coffee in the lounge. There's usually a nice fire there. I shouldn't be much longer than an hour. Then I'll drive you home – with Jackie, I hope.'

'I ... dunno ... I've never sat in a hotel lounge alone wi' a tray of coffee, Jack.'

'Oh, come on, be a devil,' Jack said with a sudden brief smile.

'All right.' She got up, followed him to the lounge, and watched with timidity while he summoned a waiter and told him to fetch coffee and after-dinner mints.

He patted her shoulder. 'I'll be as quick as I can,' he said.

His plan was simple. He intended to go the rounds of the pubs in Hotten until he spotted Tom Merrick or some pal of his. If all else failed he could ask the police for Merrick's address; they must have it, because Merrick was on bail.

Luck was with him. In the second pub he found Merrick himself. And, better still – or worse, depending on how you looked at it – Jackie was with him. It didn't matter to Merrick, apparently, that the boy was under age to be drinking in a pub.

Merrick coloured up as Jack threaded his way towards them. 'Ho, look who's here,' he remarked, tossing his head. 'We're honoured, ain't we, Jackie?'

'I've been looking for you, Merrick,' Jack said. 'Or, to be exact, for Jackie.' He looked directly at the boy. 'Your mother's worried about you, Jackie.'

'She's got no reason! If it's about that rubbish with the bike, Graham lent it to me and he'll say so.'

'But you were riding it without a licence –'

'Whose fault is that?' Jackie cut in in a belligerent tone. He had just enough beer to make him a little aggressive. 'If Mum would let me get a licence –'

'Jackie, that's not the point. You told the police you were still at the caravan.'

'Well?'

'Well, you're not.'

'What business is it of yours?' sneered Merrick. 'Who asked you to stick your nose in?'

'Pat did, as a matter of fact. But more important to you,' Jack said, having had a quick think, 'is that you're on bail and have to keep your nose clean. What're the cops going to say when they discover you've got your son staying with you although the tribunal ordered you to see him only with your wife's agreement? What are they going to say when they hear you've got him in here drinking when he's under age?'

'Oh, so you're going to rat on me, are you –'

'Not a bit. If I do, it gets everybody further into a mess. All I'm saying is –' and here he looked directly at the lad, willing him to use his brains – 'there's enough trouble as it is, without making it worse. Jackie is officially living with his mother. He's told the police he is – he's lied to them. It wouldn't take them ten minutes to find out he hasn't been home in the last four days – just supposing they called to talk to him and Sandie answered the door. Jackie, do you want Sandie to lie too? Is that your solution to your problems – involving your mother and sister in a stupidity like that?'

For a long moment there was silence among them. The background noise of the pub went on: darts thudding into the board, the muffled beat of the jukebox, the sudden giggling of a girl ...

Jack could see Tom Merrick's little wheels whirling. He was no fool. After a moment he said: 'Look, son, happen it would be a bit awkward for me if it came out you're living wi' me and Der. I mean, I 'xpect they'd say I wasn't a "fit person", wi' that charge hanging over me. An' they did make a ruling that you should stay wi' your Mum.'

'But Dad!' The boy stared at him, astounded. 'You're not sending me back?'

'Course not, Jackie. Up to you, isn't it? But you don't want to get your old man in trouble, do you?'

'Nay, I . . . ' Jackie was coming out of the fuddled state engendered by a half of bitter. He fumbled for words. 'What could they do to you, Dad?'

'Take away my bail. Put me in clink until the case in Crown Court.'

'No!'

'They could, Jackie,' Jack put in.

'I told you to stay out of trouble!' Merrick exclaimed, giving his son a glare. 'Stupid little beggar!'

'But it were only a ride on a bike, Dad!'

'That's how it seemed at the time, but it could come out a lot more than that. However, if your pal Graham is backing you up and you're living quietly at home with your mother, it may all be dropped. So what do you say, Jackie?' asked Jack.

Jackie pondered, then pushed away his empty beer mug. 'Don't have much choice, do I?'

Merrick had suddenly realised he was coming out of this badly. 'Look here, son, you don't have to do owt just because he says so. Happen it wouldn't look good if you were to be living wi' me, but you can live on your own here in Hotten – you're sixteen.'

'Wrong,' Jack said. 'The legal age for leaving home is eighteen. If Jackie's not careful, he's going to end up in a local authority home.'

'You what? Nobody's going to put my kid in a home –!'

'How would you stop them if you were in jail on remand because you'd aided a minor to disobey an injunction?'

Jackie got up. 'I've got to go, Dad,' he said. In the last few sentences Merrick had turned it around so that it looked as if he wanted his son to stay near him but was being thwarted by Clever-Dick Jack Sugden. To protect his father, Jackie had to go back to the caravan. 'Don't want to make trouble for you or me mam.'

'Now you're talking sense,' Jack said.

'We'll see each other, Dad.'

Merrick, assuming a hurt look, turned away. Jack led the way out. Without another word being spoken Jackie got into the Land-Rover. They had driven more than a mile before he said, 'This isn't the road to Beckindale.'

'We're going to collect your Mum first.'

Puzzled, Jackie sat back. He had no wish to indulge in conversation with Jack Sugden. When they drew up outside the Feathers in Connelton his expression was one of bewilderment and reluctance. Jack led the way in. Pat was sitting in the lounge with the empty silver coffee pot on a tray in front of her, her coat folded on her lap, ready to leave at a moment's notice.

Jackie didn't notice her anxiety, her look of being uncomfortable in these surroundings. All he saw was his mother, in her best dress, lolling around in a posh pub in Connelton while his father was left lonely and friendless in a sawdust bar in Hotten. He stood rigid while Pat grasped him and hugged him, exclaiming over him. When Jack said: 'Best get back, eh?' he went with them without protest.

But the look on his face as he got into the Land-Rover behind them was one of resentment bordering almost on hatred.

Chapter Seven

The atmosphere in the caravan wasn't exactly sunny after Jackie's return. He was sullen and silent. When Mr Instone came to say that the case had been dropped by the police in view of Graham Jelks's statement, he merely shrugged.

'They'll still want to talk to you.'

'Gonna give me a lecture, eh?'

'Well, you know what the fuzz is like, Jackie.' He glanced at the boy's mother hoping she would make some useful remark at this point, but Pat, who had been brought up to consider the village bobby the personification of all that was good and just, merely looked at him in surprise. 'It'd make a good impression all round if you'd settle to doing your O levels, Mac,' Instone resumed. 'How's about that, then?'

'I told you, I'm not interested. What's the point?'

'The point is you may as well do that as hang round getting into trouble,' said Instone.

'Me and my Dad were gonna start a little painting and decorating business,' Jackie muttered. 'Could've been great.'

'But did you have equipment?'

'We-ell ... we could have got it.'

'But brushes and ladders cost money, Jackie.'

'We could have got the money.'

'Where?'

'The government gives money for starting small businesses. Dad said he heard that.'

'Yes, well, there's something in that but ... '

'Dad went into the Job Centre and asked, but they wouldn't give him anything.'

Instone sighed. It was typical of the people he was trying to help that they had these absurd notions about how things worked. They heard about what they regarded as a hand-out and were sure they could get in on the act. Asking for money for a self-employed business at the Job Centre. ...! Merrick was one of those the Germans call 'half-smart', always thinking he'd found a way to easy money and always getting it wrong. What a father for a boy to have ...

'I don't think your father's going to get money to start a decorating firm, Jackie,' he said quietly. 'So it makes a lot of sense to equip yourself to get a job on your own by and by. Think what you like, kiddo, but employers don't give jobs to know-nowts. If it's between you and a chap who has proof he can spell and count and write a tidy hand, who's going to get it?'

'Aw, you're just like everybody else. I thought you were on my side!'

Instone packed away his papers and took his leave. He

81

had done all he could. Although he impressed Mrs Merrick and others unfavourably, he was quite good at his job – which was to encourage youngsters to come to terms with life as it really is, not as portrayed in the pop music magazines.

Pat was quick to see that Instone had planted a seed. The following day, a Saturday, she took them all to Leeds on a cheap ticket and let the youngsters prowl round the stores and the record shops. They even had coffee and toasted sandwiches at one of the basement 'Cellar-Gear' restaurants where rubbishy clothes and jewellery tempted in the teenagers. She made no attempt to discuss the future. But when they got back she encouraged them to say what they'd liked best among the things they'd seen.

'That big portable radio-and-cassette player,' said Jackie, roused for the time being from his sullenness.

'How much d'you think that would cost?'

'Dunno. Hundred? Hundred and twenty?'

'You have to be earning good money to be able to afford things like that.'

Jackie said nothing. Perhaps he was thinking of the contents of Derek Warne's flat, where he had stayed for the four days of his absence from home. It had had no fine record players or radio sets. No wardrobe full of trendy clothes. No carpets on the floor, even, and hardly a comfortable chair to sit in.

Its main furnishings had seemed to be empty beer cans and copies of the *Sporting Life*. There hadn't even been enough beds – Jackie had had to use a sleeping bag on the living room floor.

But that was because Derek and his Dad were on Social Security. If they'd been able to get their decorating business going . . .

As if she had been reading his mind, his sister said: 'If you ever got that decorating scheme into action, you could make a bit of money all right. There's always work for a good painter and decorator.'

'That's what I think!'

'But you have to know what you're doing, I reckon. I mean, you have to be able to do estimates so you don't come out with a loss at the end of a job. And you have to be able to keep books – unless you'd thought of moonlighting all the time and never paying any tax.'

'It was all going to be square and above board,' Jackie insisted.

Pat had caught on to what her daughter was saying. 'Seems to me a bit of education's never wasted, even if you are going to work with your hands.'

'But Mum!' protested Jackie, angry at being trapped. 'Everybody else I know has things – a decent transistor, a record-player, clothes with a bit of style to 'em . . . '

'Happen they've got parents who can earn more than I can,' she replied, her manner matter-of-fact. 'If I could get a good wage, Jackie, you'd want for nothing that ordinary lads have. But I can only get waitressing, and your Dad's never had a job in the last seven years, at least not one that he's kept for a week. If you're to have the good things, it's up to you to earn them for yourself by and by. And I don't see you doing that the way you're going on now, shirking school and being stroppy.'

The subject was dropped. Jackie slammed out in a temper. All next day, Sunday, he was in a sulk. Yet somehow it had become established that he was going to school on Monday and that he was going to work for his O levels.

'If he could just earn a few bob so he could get some of the things he puts so much store by,' Pat mourned to Jack. 'A weekend job, tha knows. But there's nothing around here.'

'Happen I could give him a few chores at Emmerdale,' Jack suggested.

She gave a quick shake of the head. 'No, Jack.'

'No?' He was puzzled. 'Why not?'

'I don't know. For some reason he doesn't want to be beholden to you. Just leave it, eh?'

'All right, you're the boss.'

He didn't understand it but if it was best that he shouldn't seem to help Jackie Merrick, he would do it by stealth. He mentioned to Joe that if there was any casual work around N.Y. Estates, Jackie was a likely candidate.

'He's good with his hands, Joe, and he really needs something to keep him out of mischief at weekends when he's not at school. Doesn't have to pay much – a couple of quid, that's all.'

'You what?' his brother said with indignation. 'His Dad tries to run me down in a van and you want me to give him a pocket money job?'

'Merrick wasn't driving the van, Joe, it was the other feller.'

Joe stopped in his stroll along the lane at Jack's side. He turned to face him. 'How do you know that?'

Jack could have bitten his tongue out. 'I ... forget. I heard it somewhere.'

'Not from me, brother! Not even from Sergeant MacArthur. As far as I can gather, they're both keeping quiet about who did what. So how do you know Merrick wasn't driving?'

'I can't tell you, Joe.'

'I see. You got it from either Jackie or Sandie Merrick. They were with me at the time. Neither of them has ever said a word to me about it – they've withheld evidence.'

'Oh, come on, Joe. You can't expect kids to give evidence that definitely ties in their father with a hit and run.'

'But you expect me to give one of them a job.'

'No,' Jack said slowly, 'I don't. I'm sorry I asked. I just thought you might want to help a kid who's in a rotten situation through no fault of his own –'

'Oh no? I haven't heard the whole of it but wasn't there something about a motorbike?'

'You never sneaked a ride on a motorbike before you had a licence, Joe?'

Joe buttoned up his sheepskin against the icy wind and turned away. 'I've got business to attend to,' he said. 'If you want my advice, you'll attend to yours.'

But Jack's last question stayed with him. Of course he'd done things he shouldn't have when he was Jackie's age. He remembered the temptation when he'd seen Emmerdale's battered old van standing with the keys in the ignition. And his first attempt at smoking ...

In the end he murmured to Richard Anstey that he'd noticed Seth Armstrong taking Jackie Merrick round to the pheasant coops from time to time. 'I gather he does quite a good job wi' making pens and that kind of thing. Y'know, Seth is always saying what a nuisance it is to him to have to come back from halfway round the estate to feed the pheasants. I was wondering . . . '

'You're saying we should give Jackie a regular job on a part-time basis? Have you spoken to Seth about it?'

'Nay, thought it'd come better from you.'

'The boy's a bit of a juvenile delinquent, though, isn't he?'

'Shouldn't think so. His Dad's a bad lot but they don't have much to do wi' him. Any road, Seth could say yes or no on that. I wouldn't imagine Seth'd let anybody near his pheasants if he thought he couldn't trust him.'

Anstey nodded dismissively. 'I'll see,' he said. He didn't really envisage giving the boy a job.

But Seth, engaged in a great campaign against the rabbits at Holly Farm, brought up the topic quite unexpectedly. 'I could do wi' someone to pop over and keep an eye on they pheasants while I'm at Holly,' he remarked. 'Won't trap many coneys if I don't keep traps emptied.' He was going to suggest that his wife would like a little pocket money. But before he could, Anstey broke in.

'It so happens I've someone in mind,' he said. 'That Merrick lad. You like having him around, don't you?'

Quickly Seth re-organised his thoughts. Happen it was better if Meg didn't have any extra money. She could prove very stubborn about parting with it, as had been shown when she earned a substantial sum with her patchwork quilts. The proceeds had gone straight into a unit trust recommended by Henry Wilks. Yes, happen Jackie Merrick was a better partner. Handy with hammer and nails and eager to learn . . . 'Yes, he's a decent lad,' he agreed.

So Jackie was hired to lend a hand to the gamekeeper of N.Y. Estates, quite unaware that the train of events had been originally set in motion by Jack Sugden. He might have refused the job if he had known.

Jack had other matters to occupy him just at present. A problem, with a faintly serious and yet comic aspect, was facing the household. Annie was due to come home from the convalescent home where she had gone on leaving hospital, but it was the generally held opinion of the younger members of the family that there could be no rest for her if Grandad were in the house.

Sam would fuss over his daughter to such an extent that, in an effort to show him she was perfectly all right, she could do herself a lot of harm. After much discussion while Sam was out of the way, Dolly had suggested it would be a good idea if Sam were to go on holiday. Everyone said, 'Yes, so it would, but it would be impossible to persuade him.' Quite so. But Dolly had taken it a stage further.

'How about if we ring his friend Seamus in Killarney and ask him to write inviting Grandad to visit him?'

'He'd never go, with Annie expected home.'

'I think he would. If we get Seamus to say he hasn't been too well – he gets bronchitis, doesn't he? He can say he's depressed and longs for company. And he can offer good fishing. Grandad will be tempted sorely – it'll appeal to his good nature and to his angling ambitions.'

'Eeh,' said Matt, 'what's your Dad's name – Machiavelli?'

'He won't go,' said Jack.

'I don't know so much,' said Joe. 'If we can get Ma to think he's giving up a lovely holiday just to be near her and if we can get her to say so and look upset . . . '

Jack looked at Matt. 'I don't think we ought to sit too close to them, Matt. They might infect us with this deviousness.'

It sounded too complicated to work, but it went like a charm after Seamus's letter arrived. Sam told Annie about it when he next visited her, because it was a nice piece of news, a letter from Seamus. There was just enough longing in his voice for Annie to say, in total innocence,

'Don't you feel you have to refuse just because I'll be coming home, Dad. I'd hate to think I'd prevented you.'

After that it took only a little urging for Sam to ring Seamus, who obligingly sounded depressed on the phone. 'You just wait, my lad,' promised Sam. 'I'll soon have you feeling yourself again.'

But Sam's trip to Ireland meant that the staff at Emmerdale was down to a very low number. And Jack was spending a lot of time – too much time, Matt privately thought – on the land he had rented from Hathersage. Loads of nitrogen-lime had to be spread on the fields now if it was to do much good, so Matt was left with almost all the normal Emmerdale routine to care for. He came for his meals looking more and more exhausted; with not even Grandad to help at milking time, Matt was at full stretch every moment of the day.

'What you need is a temporary labourer,' Joe said urgently to Jack. 'You can't go on like this, just the two of you. Ring up the Job Centre and ask them to send a couple of chaps to try them for size.'

For the next day or so, the problem was put in cold storage, as Annie came back and was made comfortable in her own home. But when she saw how short they were of help, she was beside herself. 'I'll give a hand with the milking tomorrow morning, Matt –'

'You'll do no such thing, Ma!'

'But you can't be expected to manage –'

'Dolly'll help me. The last thing you want is to slip on the cowshed floor and damage that new knee joint.'

'I should never have talked Grandad into taking that holiday!' she accused herself. 'He's needed here.'

'No he isn't,' Jack said. 'I'm ringing the Job Centre to get a temporary helper.'

The temporary helper, Jack Clayton, was shown round the farm, said he was sure he could do all they wanted, and agreed to start Monday morning. Monday morning came, no Jack Clayton. When Jack rang the Job Centre it was to learn they knew nothing about his non-appearance. They only learned what had happened by accident: Matt went into Thornton's for a spare part for the harrow and saw him there serving behind the counter. He had found himself a better-paying, permanent job, and decided not to bother with Emmerdale. He hadn't even let them know he wouldn't be coming.

'That's it, then,' Henry said when he heard about it. 'It's going to be right hard to get a man who suits and won't want a fortune for a couple of months work. I've found you someone, though.'

'Who?'

'Me.'

'You?' Jack and Matt said in chorus.

'Oh, I know I'm only an amateur at farm work, but I'm a pair of hands. I'll do whatever you tell me – the donkey jobs.'

'But Henry ... We're generally on the job by five-thirty or six.'

'Well, so shall I be.'

'Amos will adore that – you getting up and going out, disturbing him.'

'I shan't disturb him. I shan't be at the Woolpack.'

'Where will you be, then?' Matt said in mystification.

'Here, in Sam's room while he's away.'

'Henry!' Jack cried. 'It's a great idea, but what's Amos going to say?'

'He can't say anything. I told him I had decided to take a few weeks' holiday and he agreed it was only right. He's been passing me brochures about the Costa Brava for the last two days.'

Matt and Jack fell about laughing. 'I'd love to see his face when he realises you're going to the Costa Emmerdale!'

Henry fitted surprisingly well into the routine. He uncomplainingly took on whatever was allotted to him, and if he had aches in muscles whose existence was hitherto unknown to him, he never mentioned it. When Matt began work on the lambing pens, Henry hefted hurdles about with the best of them. He shovelled muck, he stacked feed and cowcake, he went on errands for spare parts, he filled bins and picked vegetables for Dolly's cooking. In the evenings he sat companionably with Annie. He tried to set aside a time each day when he would take her out for a drive and then a little walk, to get the knee joint functioning properly. He was a tower of strength.

All the same, he was as pleased as anyone when he had a chance to pause and draw breath. He was having one of those moments of peace and restoration while mending the lower field wall when Seth Armstrong came up with his shotgun draped over his arm.

'How do, Seth.'

'How do, Henry. Hard work, walling.'

'Aye, but it has to be done if we're to keep our pedigree cows where they belong.'

'Right enough. Lambing soon, eh?'

'About another week, Matt reckons.'

'Joe misses lambing, I should think. It were always one of his favourite times, and they've no need for his help wi' that on N.Y. Estates.'

'Oh, when you're on the managerial staff you don't get called out to help a ewe in trouble, I suppose.'

'Lot o' responsibility, being a manager. I wonder if it caused him much heartsearching to make that decision about Lower Puddle?'

'What decision?' Henry asked, falling straight into Seth's trap.

'You haven't heard? Happen it's just a rumour, then.'

'What rumour?' said Henry.

'Nay, if you haven't heard owt, I shouldn't talk about it. I could cause quite an upset by speaking out of turn about a big thing like that.'

'Like what?' Henry demanded. He was beginning to feel as if he were a distant echo in a cave.

'I thought . . . if the Merricks were worried about it . . . but it's just a mistake, I reckon. So long, Henry, can't stop here chatting, I've work to do if you haven't.' With that Seth sloped off, his long lunging step taking him away with amazing rapidity. Henry watched him go, baffled.

What had he just heard? That Joe – personifying N.Y. Estates – had taken, or not taken, a big decision about . . . About what? Lower Puddle Meadow. That was the field where the Merricks' caravan stood. So something was in the wind, that was clear.

He took the first opportunity of mentioning his anxiety to Jack. 'Has Mrs Merrick said owt to you about Lower Puddle field?'

'Only that it's spooky at night, when the owls hunt,' Jack replied with a laugh. And then, with his hand on its way to his mouth with a large slice of home-made bread, 'What about Lower Puddle?'

'Been left fallow a long time, hasn't it?'

'Aye, four years,' Matt put in. 'They had two other 'vans there for temporary workers so they've let it go.'

The men looked at each other. 'When you come to think of it,' Henry said, 'it seems out of character for N.Y. Estates to leave a good piece of land lying useless.'

'Aye,' Matt said.

Annie, pouring tea, frowned to herself. 'What makes you ask, Henry?'

'It was just summat I heard.'

'What about?'

'About some decision N.Y. Estates have made.'

'Decision? What sort of decision?'

'Happen it's just a rumour,' Henry replied, and thought, 'I sound like Seth.'

'What rumour?'

'Nay, it may be nothing,' Henry said, wondering how he had ever got into this conversation again. But Jack was exchanging glances with Matt.

'If N.Y. Estates have decided to bring Lower Puddle into use, it could make a heck of a difference to Pat Merrick and her kids.'

'I suppose it could.'

'Has Pat said anything to you?' Matt asked of Jack.

'Nay, but I haven't seen her in a while. We've been so busy with our new land and so on.'

'It'd be a kindness to see if anything is happening there,' Annie told him. 'I mean, she doesn't have many people to turn to ... '

It was a good thing her father wasn't here to hear her say that. The last thing he wanted was to hear Jack being urged to befriend Pat Merrick. But Annie had known troubles of her own when she would have welcomed help and advice. Her dead husband Jacob, while nothing like the hapless Tom Merrick, had caused her much anxiety in her time and her sympathy was more with Pat than Sam would have thought justified.

Jack finished his tea and put on his jacket. 'Just going for a quick visit to the Merricks,' he said, and hurried out.

Pat was delighted to see him. The family had finished their evening meal, the table was cleared, and Sandie was immersed in algebra homework. Jackie too was doing homework, but he rose and went into his bedroom at Jack's arrival. Jack thought nothing to it; the boy wanted to get on with his reading without interruption.

'Can I get you a cup of tea, Jack?'

'Nay, lass, I've just had mine. Listen, have you heard anything about plans to use Lower Puddle?'

Pat stared at him. 'Funny you should say that. Our Jackie was just saying that there seems to be summat afoot.'

'Such as what?'

'I don't know exactly. What did he say, Sandie?'

Sandie looked up from her algebra. 'Was it that Mr Anstey had been looking at the field?'

'He saw Mr Anstey?'

'I don't think so,' Pat said. 'I . . . don't really remember. Jackie?' she called.

'What?'

'Come in a minute, love. What was it you heard bout the field?'

Jackie put an unwilling head round the bedroom door. 'I'm trying to do history, Mum!'

'But you said you'd heard something was mebbe going to be done?'

Jackie grunted. 'Mr Anstey seems to be looking at the land.'

'You saw him?'

'No, I heard he'd been walking round it. I saw his car in the lane yesterday, though.' He sighed. 'Can I get on now?' If he had been more willing to sit and talk, it would have been clear that his information came from Seth Armstrong, who had told him about Anstey's actions while they were feeding the pheasants the previous day. Not that it mattered who spread the word in the first place – the news would have got around some time. But it later became clear that Seth had made sure the whole of Beckindale knew of Anstey's plans at the very outset.

'It's a bit worrying, isn't it?' Pat said to Jack. 'If they decide to use this field, we'll have to move out.'

'I'll go straight and talk to Joe about it,' Jack said, and jumped up.

'It's nice of you to bother,' Pat said. 'I'd feel easier in my mind.'

'I'll let you know.'

Joe was at Demdyke, eating a very large sandwich with a bowl of soup. When he had let his brother in, he returned to his food, his stockinged feet on the opposite chair. 'To what do I owe the honour of this visit?'

'Listen, Joe, is it true you're going to put Lower Puddle Meadow into use again?'

Joe took his feet off the chair and sat up straight. 'Who the devil told you that?' he asked.

'Never mind who told me. It's true, then?'

'No, it isn't as it happens.'

'You're not going to do anything in that area?'

'I didn't say that.'

'You are going to do something? What?'

'I don't see that it's any business of yours, Jack–'

'Oh, come on, Pat Merrick and her family live there. Anything that happens to Lower Puddle Meadow is important.'

Joe took a deep breath and let it out. 'Well,' he said, 'I don't see any reason to keep it a dark secret, though I'd like to know how you got hold of it so soon. N.Y. Estates are going to plough up Upper Puddle for feed grain.'

'Upper Puddle?'

'Aye, so you see, your anxiety about the Merricks isn't needed. Their field isn't going to be touched.'

Jack was silent, his mind busy. At Joe's first words he'd

felt a bit of a fool, but now he began to see what the news implied. 'But ... if you plough up Upper Puddle, you plough up the footpath.'

'I don't know about that.'

'What d'you mean, you don't know about that? That area of N.Y.'s property is your sphere of control, isn't it?'

'Well, as a matter of fact ... ' And Joe frowned.

'What?'

'Richard took Ridge Farm from me at the end of last week and gave me Blea Slope Farm instead.' He pushed away his soup-bowl. He was deep in thought.

'In other words,' said Jack, 'he foresaw that you wouldn't go along with ploughing up a footpath so he gave you something else to look after instead.'

'Nay, I don't know that that's true, Jack –'

'I'm not having this,' Jack said. 'In the first place, he's no right to plough up a footpath and in the second, if he got away with it, Pat would have to walk all the long way round by the alley and Ridge Lane to get to her caravan.'

'Listen, Jack, I'm by no means sure that you've got this right. All I know for sure is that Richard's got plans to use Upper Puddle and he's been looking at the survey maps. It's true the footpath goes through Upper Puddle, but it may only be a right of way – so long as he leaves room to walk round the field after it's ploughed, he's fulfilled his legal obligations.'

'That footpath's been there ever since I can remember –'

'But there's no saying it's more than a right of way, Jack.'

'Custom and tradition have a lot to do with it, and you know by tradition that's always been a path –'

'Listen, I don't want to discuss it any more. It's nowt to do wi' me. If you want to take it up, you'll have to speak to Richard Anstey.'

'Washing your hands, are you, Joe?'

Joe gave his brother a weary glance. 'Go away,' he said. 'I was in the middle of my tea when you arrived, after a

93

hard day's work. If you want to have a row with somebody, choose another sparring partner.'

Angrily Jack stalked to the door. 'You can't chicken out of it just because he transferred you to look after Blea Slope. You're part of Beckindale, Joe, and you have a responsibility –'

'Get lost,' Joe said, and turned his head away as his brother slammed out of the cottage.

He ate the remains of his sandwich, debating whether to get in touch with Richard. But Richard was at a dinner in Bradford, safe out of Jack's reach, so what was the need to call him away from his soup and duck à l'orange? The morning would be time enough to let him know of this hornet's nest that was buzzing.

Joe was not looking forward to next day, in any case. He had to go to Hotten to give evidence in the case against Tom Merrick.

He was up at Home Farm next day well before the sun got there. Richard was still eating breakfast. 'You're an early bird,' he remarked, waving his hand at the coffee pot in invitation. Joe shook his head and sat down opposite him. Anstey eyed him. 'What's to do?'

Joe tapped the folded map on the table in front of Anstey's plate. 'Been studying up on the terrain?'

Anstey raised his eyebrows. 'Why not?'

'Lower Puddle field is where Pat Merrick's 'van stands.'

'Of course. It's the edge of Ridge Farm. I've taken a good look and there's no problem there. When John Tuplin ploughs Potts Bank he can do Upper Puddle, without ever disturbing the Merricks.'

Joe hesitated. 'But there's the path. Lower Puddle Path goes over Upper Puddle, you know –'

'Of course I know, Joe. I've been studying the map, haven't I?'

'Then you've been studying what the reaction's likely to be, I should think. How're the Merricks to get to their 'van?'

'They'll still have their right of way –'

'Over a ploughed field?!'

'They won't have to walk over furrows, Joe, you know that well enough. They can go round the headland. I'll tell Tuplin to leave a good headland on the west perimeter and up here to the point where it enters the copse. I can't see how anyone can grumble at that.'

Joe looked at him. Anstey met his glance with a bland smile. 'Is this why you took me off Ridge Farm and gave me Blea Slope to manage?'

'What's the difference? One farm is very much like another, isn't it?' Anstey collected up his breakfast things and left them for his daily to wash. Over the clatter he added, 'Is this why you arrived so early? To discuss a little thing like ploughing Upper Puddle?'

Joe shrugged. 'It isn't a little thing, and you know it, Richard. You'll have them about your ears any minute now. I thought I'd better sound the alarm before I go into Hotten for the trial.'

'Oh yes, the trial. You've made arrangements for Mason to handle any problems while you're there?' At Joe's nod he went on, 'How long do you think it'll take?'

'Heaven knows. You know what court proceedings are like,' Joe groaned.

But in fact the trial of Tom Merrick and Derek Warne, which had attracted quite a crowd of spectators from not only Hotten but surrounding villages, was almost spectacularly short. When the prisoners were asked: 'How do you plead?' each answered, 'Guilty, my lord.' A sigh, perhaps of disappointment, went round the public benches. They'd been hoping for a bit of a drama, with Joe Sugden in the witness box describing whatever it was that Warne and Merrick had done to him.

The Crown Court judge addressed each man in turn. Neither of them could exactly have enjoyed the experience, but a stolid expression hides most emotions. Mr Justice Cairns told them that they had been reckless and ill-intentioned, careless of life and property. He sentenced them each to twelve months but, in view of the fact that this was the first time they had ever been involved in serious crime, he suspended the sentence on condition of good behaviour during the time of its validity. He ended with a warning that they seemed to be a bad influence on each other and recommended that they should avoid each other's company.

He then watched with a disillusioned eye while the two men grinned at each other in jubilation, clearly convinced that they had put one over on the Law. Joe, too, observed them leave the building and thought they looked more like men who had been declared innocent rather than guilty. But if it meant he didn't have to stand up in court and submit to cross-questioning, he was not going to complain.

All the same, it gave him no pleasure to think that Tom Merrick had been let loose on the world again.

Chapter Eight

Joe's fears for Beckindale's peace of mind would have been justified next morning if he had seen Tom Merrick thumbing a lift from Hotten. He arrived in the village about eight o'clock of a bright, cold spring morning, knowing very well that he'd find Jackie at the pheasant coops because this was Saturday. He'd had a couple of short letters from his son since Jack Sugden persuaded him to abide by the conditions of the tribunal's ruling and stay away from Tom.

Jackie was mending a hole that might have been made by a fox. The netting was bent and the earth beneath it a little scooped out. But luckily the fox hadn't been able to get in among the helpless hen pheasants. Tom said: 'Morning, son.'

Jackie turned on his knees. ''Lo, Dad.'

'Heard about the result of the case, did you?'

'Aye, it was all round Hotten by school dinner-time yesterday.'

'Your mates give you a hard time?'

Jackie coloured up. 'They said ... you wouldn't have pleaded guilty if you were innocent.'

'Nay, Jackie ... ' Merrick had given a lot of thought to how to handle this. His son was a fundamentally honest and law-abiding lad, so Merrick had to have a good reason for what he'd done. He used the one which had worked with his lawyer.

'Sitha, lad, Christmas was coming on and I wanted to have some cash to give you and Sandie a bit of a present. It's hard on a man when he's parted from his kids and can't have a happy time at Christmas wi' them.'

'Aye, but –'

'Christmas trees,' Merrick swept on. 'It's not as if I took summat that belonged to somebody. I didn't snatch some old lady's handbag, now did I?'

'No, but –'

'Trees just grow, Jackie – I mean, you must have gathered blackberries a thousand times without saying to yourself, I'm stealing these from Mr Hathersage's land.'

'But blackberries grow wild, Dad. Those trees –'

'I know, I know, they were in a plantation. I'm not saying it was right to take 'em. But it's not stealing ... I didn't take Mr Anstey's car or Seth's gun – I took some trees that nobody was going to miss – '

'But you got money for them –'

'Of course I did. I wanted to give you and Sandie something for Christmas. I couldn't have done much wi' what I had in my pocket –'

'But Joe Sugden –'

'Now, Jackie, be fair. That weren't me. That were Derek – and you know what a daft beggar Derek is.'

'But you did take the trees and do a lot of damage –'

'And that's why I pleaded guilty, son. Be fair – I stood up and took my medicine, didn't I?' Only after his lawyer had told him he'd get off lightly by doing so and enlisting the leniency of the court – but he didn't mention that.

'Aye, that's true –'

'I knew it would mean some hard words from your pals, lad. But there's some things a man has to do.' He stifled a grin. He could hear the phrase from the spaghetti

Westerns: a man's gotta do what a man's gotta do. But luckily Jackie was too confused to recall it too.

'Well, I see that,' Jackie said. 'Yes, I know you wouldn't have made us a talking shop if you hadn't had to. But it's all over now, thank goodness.'

'What's your Mum been saying about it?'

'She doesn't talk about it much, Dad. She's kind of quiet these days.'

'Doesn't go out much?'

'Only with –' Jackie bit off the words. He wouldn't tell his father that his mother had a man friend. It sounded somehow ... cheap. 'She's worried about this plan of N.Y. Estates.'

'What's that, then?' Merrick was always interested in anything to do with N.Y. Estates. As the biggest land-owner in the dale, they were a source of income in many ways.

'Seems they're gonna plough up our footpath. It'll be rotten if they do. A long walk round by the alley and Ridge Lane, and no lights on it in the dark, not to mention it's got no surface once you get to the fields.'

'Ploughing up Lower Puddle Path? Can they do that?'

'Seth says Mr Wilks says they can't.'

'Anybody doing owt?'

'Jack Sugden's talked to his brother about it, I gather. No go.'

'Nay, you'd not expect Jack Sugden to go agin his own brother, now would you.'

'I think he really wants to stop the ploughing up. He seems to be hot on preserving old rights.' Jackie had to give the man his due. Little though he liked him, he really was bestirring himself about the footpath.

He finished the work on the wire netting and got to his feet. Now he had to throw grain for the hens. He went to fetch it from the shed. His father moved along with him. 'What you doing these days, lad, besides acting nursemaid to the pheasants?'

'Oh, school, you know ... I'm ... I'm going to work for O Level English and history.'

'Good for you.' Jackie looked at him in surprise, and

Merrick went on: 'I've been made to think on, Jackie. Happen I'd have made more of my life if I'd paid more heed to my schooling.'

'Oh ... well..'

'What d'you do in your spare time? Go out with pals?'

'Well, Graham Jelks comes over now and then. And Andy Longthorn – but he's Sandie's friend, really.'

'Boy-friend, eh?'

'Sort of.'

'Speaking of which ... Anybody else come round a lot?'

'No.'

'Jack Sugden?'

Jackie shook his head vehemently. It was something he didn't want to think about. Moreover, it was the strict truth to say Jack wasn't often at their home. Jack had been very busy with work on the farm for weeks past.

'I thought he was a good friend,' Merrick said with scorn. 'To your mam, I mean. They go back a long way together.'

'Aye, well ... She doesn't go out much but if she does ... It's usually Jack Sugden who takes her.' Before his eyes rose his memory of his mother in her best dress at the Feathers. 'What she sees in him–!'

'No accounting for tastes, is there, lad?' Merrick said, slapped him on the shoulder, and walked off.

So ... During the weeks of his bail, when good sense had dictated he keep away from Beckindale, Jack Sugden had been taking advantage. Typical, that was. Wait till a man was hampered by stupid legal red tape, and then get cuddly with his wife ...

But bail was over, the case was over, and the suspended sentence could be disregarded so long as he kept his nose clean as far as the law was concerned. 'Good conduct' – that meant only in the legal sense. Nobody said you had to let some smart alec walk off with your wife.

He gave it some thought for the next couple of hours. He had to be seen to be as pure as the driven snow. Right, he'd enlist himself on the side of the angels straight away.

A 'good cause' lay ready to hand. He went to the verger of the parish church and inquired if the parish hall was available for a public meeting a week from today.

'A meeting, Tom Merrick?' said old Josh Potter with incredulity. 'What's thee want a meeting for?'

'Never you mind. Can I book the hall?'

'I have to know the reason afore I can book it.'

'Protest meeting about the footpath destruction.'

Potter was taken aback. He himself was full of protest about that. 'What's thee gettin' involved for?'

'My missus is goin' to have to walk half a mile round the fields every time she goes out, that's what for,' Merrick said. 'Yes or no, can I book the hall?'

'How you goin' to pay the hire?'

'Public donations at the meeting.'

'Huh. One pound booking fee, Tom Merrick.' He held out a horny hand.

Swearing inwardly, Merrick produced a pound note. Never mind, he'd get it back somehow. And if he didn't, it was worth it.

Laboriously Potter inscribed his name in the bookings ledger with a note alongside. 'Purpose, to oppose footpath destruction.' There, thought Merrick, if ever there was clear evidence of his reformation, this was it.

He had already planned the next move. He went into the Woolpack as soon as it opened at eleven to take up his watch there. Amos eyed him askance but he had bought a half and intended to buy another if need be. Amos couldn't complain that he didn't spend any money. He could, of course, have carried out Stage Two by walking to N.Y.'s fields – but he wanted this event to happen in public.

By and by his patience was rewarded. At about eleven forty-five Richard Anstey came in with Joe Sugden. Merrick knew they generally toasted the arrival of the weekend by a drink in the pub on Saturday morning. He waited until they had ordered their drinks then walked up to them. He didn't actually touch his forelock, but there was something of that in his manner.

'Mr Anstey. Joe.' He gave each a nod. They regarded

him warily. 'I just wanted to say ... I know you think badly of me, but I've learned my lesson. I'm sorry for what I did.'

He hung his head and looked contrite. Anstey cleared his throat. 'Er ... well ... '

'I didn't think, you see. I mean, them trees were just ... standing there. But I'm sorry, and more so for the damage we did. That weren't me,' he put in hastily. 'Derek had the saw, not me.'

'I notice he's not here, apologising,' Anstey remarked.

'No, well, he's not got a family, has he? I've had time to think and I realise what a fool I've been to myself and my family, Mr Anstey. I apologise.' He turned to Joe, who had been gazing at him as if he had two heads. 'And I apologise even more for what Derek did wi' that van, Joe. I were horrified at the time and I look back on it and wonder how I ever let myself in for a thing like that. I hope you accept what I say.'' He held out his hand.

Joe would have liked to sink through the earth. The last thing he wanted was to shake hands with Tom Merrick, whom he wouldn't have trusted any further than he could throw a combine harvester. But the eyes of the others in the bar were upon them, and how could he refuse? He shook hands and muttered: 'All right.'

Amos was beside himself with curiosity. He wished Mr Wilks was there to be nudged and whispered at. But Mr Wilks was still dwelling at Emmerdale 'on holiday'. So Amos was quite pleased when Merrick came up to the bar and asked for a refill.

'Er ... glad the court case is behind you, I s'pose,' he ventured as he pulled the beer.

'Aye. Daft, that were. Can't think how I ever got into it.'

'Mr Anstey quite content to let bygones be bygones?'

'Oh aye. I have to give him his due. He's give my lad a part-time job and my missus a place to live. Seems funny a feller with a good heart like that can do this thing wi' Puddle Path.'

'Aye, everybody's talking about that,' Amos agreed.

'They'll have more to talk about by and by,' Merrick promised him. 'Just play your cards right wi' me, Amos, and you'll have an exclusive story for the *Courier*.'

'What?' Amos cried. 'About the footpath?'

'Aye.' Merrick closed one eye and looked knowing.

'What do you know about t'footpath?'

'Enough to be sure folk don't want it to go, lad. I'll tell you more next time I come in. So long, Amos.'

For the first time that he could ever recall, Amos was sorry that Tom Merrick drank up and went out.

Merrick's next port of call was the Market Cafe in Hotten. He knew by prior enquiry that Pat was on nine till five today. He went in and queued up for a hot pie and a cup of tea. Pat, pushing a little trolley laden with clean plates to the counter, saw him and looked away, distressed.

'I want a word with you, lass,' Tom said, leaning round the glass display on the counter.

'I can't, Tom. I'm busy.'

'Don't get a lunch break?'

'Well ... yes ... but I –'

'I'll wait for you outside.'

'No, I generally just have a cup of tea and a sandwich in the kitchens.'

'Outside,' Tom said. 'It's important.'

Rather than have an argument here, she nodded. She couldn't take her break until the greater part of the lunchtime crowd had gone, so it was just after two when she came out. Tom had been standing in the doorway of a nearby tobacconist, waiting. He joined her at once, cheerful and uncomplaining about having stood in the cold for an hour.

'Had your lunch?' he inquired with concern.

'No, I thought ... '

'Come on, I'll buy you a sandwich.'

He led her to a sandwich bar in Golden Lane. Here too the lunchtime rush was over so they settled on stools in a corner and were almost alone.

'I wanted to say, Pat,' he began, looking boyish and ashamed, 'that I'm sorry it's been such a mess between

102

us. I know it's been my fault. It's taken a thing like standing in front of a judge to show me what a fool I've been.'

Pat Merrick looked into the frank, pleading eyes and thought: here we go again. But she couldn't find anything to say.

'I never really meant harm to anyone. Especially not to you and the kids.'

He looked at her expectantly. Still she made no reply. This wasn't going as well as he expected. Generally she began to melt about now.

'I don't blame you if you don't want to talk to me. I deserve it.'

Pat stirred her coffee.

'I hear you've been seeing Jack Sugden,' he said with a sigh.

'Who told you that?'

'Oh.' He shrugged. 'You know the way people talk.'

'Jack has tried to be a friend, Tom.'

'That's what I said. He's a nice feller, I've got nowt against him.'

She sighed. 'What are you up to, Tom?'

'I'm not up to anything. Look, on the level, I've had my lesson. When it looked like I was going to do a twelve month sentence before the judge announced it was suspended. ... It really scared me, Pat. I've never been the sort that's liked being cooped up, now have I?'

'That's true enough,' she agreed. And if there was a shadow of bitterness in the words, that meant she knew he didn't like being cooped up in a marriage, he missed it.

'I made up my mind there and then that it was time to start mending my ways.' He smiled. 'Not as if I've much choice, have I? Put a foot wrong and they've got me! In I go, behind bars.'

Pat nodded, watching him. It struck him that she was staying very cool and detached. It was as if she had put up a guard against him.

All he could do was go on with his story. It ought to melt the iciest heart, he thought. 'I'm going all out to find a job now, Pat. A proper steady job, if I can find anybody as'll take me on after the fool I've made of meself.'

'Jobs aren't easy to come by, Tom. Not in Hotten or nearby.'

'But I want it to be nearby, love. So as to be near the kids ... and you.'

By now she should have been blushing with embarrassment and a sense of having misjudged him. But she simply sat in silence then took a sip at the coffee.

'You can see what I'm getting at, Pat?' he pleaded. 'If I can get a job and straighten myself out, happen get a decent place to live ... '

'What?' she asked, suddenly looking up with a gaze full of apprehension.

He gave her a look full of humble entreaty.

'If I can show you I mean to do better, will you take me back, lass?'

Chapter Nine

Jack Sugden was deep in discussion with his family about whom to approach on the subject of the footpath when the phone rang. It was Pat Merrick.

'Jack, could I see you later this evening?'

He was surprised. He'd intended to pay a visit to the vicar over the footpath problem. But he recovered himself. 'Summat wrong, Pat?'

'Tom's been arguing with me ... '

'About what?'

'I can't stop to discuss it now, Jack, or I'm going to miss my bus. I'm in the phonebox at Hotten Market Square.'

'All right then. What if I come by at eight o'clock and we go to the Woolpack?'

'Righto, Jack. And ... thanks.'

Jack was puzzled. Joe had told him about the scene of repentance in the Woolpack at lunchtime – as unlikely an event as an income tax refund.

'If you ask me,' Joe had said, 'he's up to something, but I dunno what.'

They had been amicable with each other, the two brothers. Jack had realised he was unfair in expecting Joe to be able to do anything about the plans for Upper Puddle field. He understood now that Anstey had had written instructions from his board of management to bring that sector into production and had done the best he could in the circumstances by taking on the responsibility himself, removing it from Joe's shoulders.

'What puzzles me,' Joe had murmured, 'is how he came to be so clumsy as to let it get out before he had the work done.'

'You mean it wouldn't have mattered if he'd ploughed up the path first and let us know later?'

'You know what I mean, Jack. Folk accept a fait accompli a lot easier than summat they know about in advance.'

'Aye,' Jack had agreed, 'it does seem funny he let us all get to know his intentions.'

His mother had gathered that the phone call was from Pat Merrick. 'You'll not be seeing Mr Hinton then?' she inquired.

'I'll fit that in too. I can go there on my way to collect Pat.' He sighed, shaking his head. 'The trouble is, I think the vicar may quote that bit at me – how does it go? "Render unto Caesar the things that are Caesar's" ... That field does belong to N.Y. Estates, there's no denying it. And you can understand it's a nuisance to them, if they want to use it – a gurt slice taken out of the middle for a footpath.'

'Nowt o't'sort!' Henry objected. He felt strongly on the subject. As a keen birdwatcher he valued the footpaths because without them it would have been much more difficult to get to good terrain. Besides, he was a Beckindaler by adoption now; whatever harmed the village harmed Henry. 'You go and see if you can get Mr Hinton to head a group who'll send in a letter protesting about the plan. I'll sign, and I bet almost everybody else will!'

Hinton was as perturbed as everyone else, but for different reasons. He foresaw argument and dissension among his parishioners. He said to Jack: 'What proof do we have that Richard Anstey really intends to destroy the footpath, Jack?'

'Joe asked him. He says Anstey's had instructions from head office.'

'And there will be no access across the field?'

'Oh aye, the right of way will remain. Anstey wants us all to trudge round the outside edge.'

'All?' Hinton said, raising his eyebrows. He knew as well as Jack did that not very many people used the path. The Merricks, Seth Armstrong on his way to Swinney Copse to look after his pheasant pens, Mr Wilks when out walking, Mrs Midgeley who lived in Old Bower Cottage at the far end of Ridge Lane and the vicar himself when he went visiting her. . . . You couldn't call it a huge number of people inconvenienced by the changing of the route.

Jack explained Henry's idea of a letter of complaint. 'Would you be willing to organise it?'

The vicar thought about it. 'I don't exactly know whether I feel strongly enough about it to appear as the . . . the initiator. But if the village wants a letter to be sent I'm certainly prepared to go round inviting signatures.'

'You're not against it, in other words?'

'I shall go along with the wishes of the majority of the community. This is a community matter.'

Jack could have wished to hear him sound less dispassionate, but thanked him and left. He drove to the edge of the field over which there was now so much discussion and in the dark took the footpath. It was certainly much more pleasant to walk across the centre of the meadow than to have to go round in the darkness by the hedge. That could be quite unpleasant, he thought, on a moonless night.

Pat was ready when he tapped on the door. She stepped out, calling back to her children that she wouldn't be long. When Jack took her arm to escort her to the Land-Rover, she seemed to grasp him tightly.

'Trouble?'

'He came to the cafe this afternoon. He was ... quite different from his usual self. Said he was sorry for the past and wanted to ... make amends. Jack, he asked me to take him back!'

Jack was startled. Her voice was strained and unhappy. She couldn't have agreed? The idea struck at him like a blow. 'What did you say?'

'I didn't know what to say! I were that astonished ... I got away on pretext that I was late getting back – this was in my lunch break.'

'But you must have said something?'

'I said it took me by surprise –'

'"This is so sudden",' Jack murmured, with wry amusement.

'Don't joke, love. This is serious. He's up to something. I'm sure he knows I won't go back to him. To tell the truth, I sometimes think he were quite glad to be shot of me when I left. I *had* turned into a nag, I know that. And say what he likes now, he never took any real interest in the kids. Now all of a sudden he's telling me everything'll be different, he'll get a job and stay out of trouble ... '

'You don't believe he means it.'

'Not Tom. He wouldn't change his ways, not for a king's ransom. So why's he bothering to tell me a tale like that?'

'I don't know so much, Pat. It sometimes hits a man,' Jack said, knowing the truth of the words, 'that time's going by and he's missing out on the important things in life ... Happen Tom's come to his senses.'

'He hasn't any senses to come to!'

They laughed, and as they reached the Land-Rover the sense of strain vanished. He handed her in and got in himself, then started the motor. As they moved off he said: 'Are you asking my advice?'

'On whether to take him up on his offer? Oh no. My mind's made up on that, has been for a long time.'

'Then what?'

'I wanted an opinion. What do you think he's up to?'

Jack shook his head. The workings of Tom Merrick's mind were beyond him.

It somehow seemed inevitable that the first person they should see as they entered the bar was Tom Merrick himself, sitting at a table with a sheet of paper in front of him. He looked up as they came in. It so happened that they were hand in hand. For a moment the expression on his face was frightening, but no one noticed – all eyes were turned to see Jack Sugden escorting Pat Merrick yet again, just to show Beckindale that the first time hadn't been a mistake.

Amos was agog. Here they were, coming in together as if they didn't care who saw them. And there was Tom Merrick at a table the far side of the room. Amos turned to look at Merrick. But Merrick was busy with a thick red pen on a sheet of paper he'd brought with him. Quiet enough, thank heaven. Reassured, Amos turned back to his new customers.

'Pint, please, Amos, and a vodka and orange. Busy tonight.'

'Always busy Saturday,' Amos said as he filled the order.

'Amos don't care whether he's got customers or not,' Seth Armstrong put in. 'He's got other things on his mind.'

'That right, Amos?'

'That's his way of saying I'm composing my piece for the *Courier* on how N.Y. Estates is taking away Beckindale's rights on t'footpath.' Amos sounded lofty, as befitted an author.

'Oh aye, that'll make a good piece for you, won't it. I hope the vicar'll be taking round a letter for us all to sign.'

'Oh? I hadn't heard that.'

'You'll hear more in a few days. Mr Hinton wants to find out how strong the feeling is.'

'How's he going to find that out?' Amos inquired.

'He'll go round and ask 'em, Amos,' Seth said. 'He's got a tongue in his head, tha knows.'

'It'll take him a while, won't it?'

At that moment, by sheer coincidence, Tom Merrick got up and went to the notice board which was a feature of the Woolpack bar. He raised his sheet of paper, lettered in red, and found a drawing pin with which to fix it.

'Hi!' cried Amos in indignation. 'What you doing wi' my board?'

'Putting a notice on it,' Tom said over his shoulder.

'You need my permission to do that,' Amos declared. 'Bring it here.'

Without hesitation Merrick obeyed. He handed the paper to Amos. There was just the slightest glint of a glance towards Jack as he said: 'Can't deny it's summat as should be done by someone wi' a bit of concern for our rights, now can you?'

Amos had cast a quick eye over the wording, his mouth falling open. He frowned then shrugged. 'Nay, you're right ... You can put it up.'

Merrick went back to the notice board, pinned up his paper, and stood back. Others crowded forward to read what was written. In large red capitals they read: LOWER PUDDLE PATH – Protest Meeting – Village Hall – Next Saturday – 8pm.

There was a murmur of approval. One or two actually clapped Merrick on the back. He turned away, and came almost face to face with Jack Sugden, who had paused on his way to Pat with her drink. For a moment they stood looking at each other.

Then with a little smile Merrick nodded and moved to the door.

In the meantime the verger, who was not on the telephone, had bethought himself that he ought to tell the vicar about the hiring of the hall. The hall was used for all sorts of meetings – Women's Institute, adult education, dog training, committee meetings, choir practice ... Yet Josh Potter was uneasy. He had never hired out the hall to a villain like Tom Merrick before.

Mr Hinton, on hearing the news, was astounded. 'Tom Merrick?'

'Yes, vicar.'

'Did he pay the booking deposit?'

'Yes, vicar, and says he'll get the rest by taking up a collection at the meeting.'

'Ye-es,' said Hinton. He had no doubt that he would collect enough to pay. More than enough, probably. Left to themselves the villagers might not have done much more than grumble. But summoned to a public meeting, they would make their voices heard. They would turn up in large numbers and make speeches. Tom Merrick could be sure of getting enough for the hiring – but why was he bothering?

Hinton didn't know Merrick well. He had come to Beckindale after the Merrick family moved to Hotten, and all he had learnt of them was through occasional mentions in the newspapers and from gossip unwillingly received. But nothing he had heard had made him think of Merrick as a champion of human rights. What could be behind it?

When Jack came home with the news to Emmerdale, puzzlement there was just as profound. Dolly said: 'It's a scheme to do somebody down. Tom Merrick never did a public-spirited thing in his life.'

Even Matt, who never had a bad word to say for anyone, nodded in agreement. 'It's a queer business.'

'I think we have to give the man credit,' Henry said. 'He's taken action while all the rest of us were just sitting round muttering.'

'You think it's the right action, Henry?' Annie inquired.

'A public meeting? Can't be anything wrong in that.'

She said no more. But there was a look of doubt in her eyes that stayed with him. Next day, while he was taking her out for her obligatory walk – what she referred to as her 'dog-training' – he said: 'What do you think should be done about this footpath business?'

'It wants some thought, doesn't it?'

'You're not in favour of the public meeting? I rather thought that was a good notion of Merrick's. I never thought I'd ever have a good word to say for the feller, but you have to give him his due – he took immediate action while we were just talking.'

'Aye,' she said in a dry tone.

'What does that mean?'

110

She paused before replying. 'I don't know what his intentions were, Henry. All I know is this. At a protest meeting, what you get is protests.'

'Well, of course . . . '

'Voices get raised, people accuse other people.'

'Well, we have summat to accuse N.Y. Estates of – they're taking away our footpath.'

'I'm not saying that isn't true. But it doesn't really matter to Tom Merrick, now does it?'

'His wife and children live –'

'They live there because Richard Anstey gave them the place. How d'you think Tom really feels about that? He showed how he felt, I'd say, when he robbed them of fifty or sixty valuable Christmas trees. And what happened then, Henry?'

'About the trees? Well, Merrick was charged and . . . ' His voice died away.

'Think on,' Annie said. 'Happen we do need a meeting to decide what to do about t'footpath. But if you want my opinion, Merrick's called it because he knows it'll embarrass N.Y. Estates.'

Henry went pink at his own stupidity in having failed to think this out for himself. He thought about it now, and gave his opinion. 'You may be right, but isn't it all to the good if N.Y. Estates are embarrassed?'

Annie said nothing.

'You don't think so?'

'When you were in business, Henry, did you make a point of embarrassing business colleagues you had to deal with?'

'Oh.' Another silence. 'Happen it's a bit tactless of me to be so quick to side with Merrick. What you're saying is, he's using Beckindale to get back at N.Y. Estates.'

'I don't know for sure. That may not be his reason . . . It just seems a likely possibility to me. Another thing might be that he's trying to give the impression of being completely reformed. That business about a public apology to Richard, and shaking Joe's hand in the Woolpack.'

'Well, Annie, I'd have thought you'd agree with all that!'

'I'm more inclined to think well of those who do good by stealth, lad. But happen this activity about the footpath is just another way of telling everybody he's a good boy now.'

'Could be. I still don't see the harm in it, Annie.'

'You're quite happy to have Tom Merrick organising this protest?'

'Well, he's not doing it on his own . . . '

'Who's with him? Who's the committee? Who's going to be on the platform?'

Henry gaped. 'I've no idea.'

'Nor have I. Henry, working at Emmerdale has made you so tired your brain's stopped functioning. Ask yourself. Do you really want an important event to be in the hands of the likes of Tom Merrick?'

Henry shook his head. 'But that's the way things are. I can't wrench it away from him.'

'But do you have to let him be the only one taking action?'

'You mean . . . take steps on my own initiative?'

'Why not? Tom Merrick did. Why should he have all the leadership qualities all of a sudden?'

They turned and began to walk back to Henry's car. For a few minutes he busied himself with inquiring whether the walk had tired her and whether her knee felt all right. When he had settled her in and they were on their way home, he said, 'You've given this a lot more thought than I have. What would your move be?'

'A quiet word with Richard Anstey.'

'What, you mean, go behind Merrick's back?'

'Since when do we have to consult Tom Merrick before we take a step?'

'Aye, you're right, but it sort of seems like . . . consorting wi' the enemy.'

'But that's just the point, Henry. Richard isn't an enemy. That notice about the protest meeting has had the effect of making us feel he *is* one.'

'By heck, Annie! If you're right . . . '

'If I'm right we're being led over the edge of Lipper's Leap. Seems to me we should draw back afore we hurt ourselves.'

'Right, lass! I'll give it some thought.'

Henry had seen Anstey in church that morning so knew he hadn't gone away for the day as he sometimes did on Sundays. He rang him from Emmerdale asking to be spared a few minutes. Anstey replied with perfect civility that he'd be pleased to give Henry a cup of tea if he cared to call. He was equally friendly and forthcoming when Henry broached the subject of the footpath.

'I've had written instructions,' he said. 'The letter's in the study – you can see it if you like. It's no choice of mine. In fact, I argued against it, because I felt it would be an embarrassment to Joe. I don't want anything to upset Joe's relations with the top brass. He has a great career ahead of him with N.Y. Estates.'

Despite himself, Henry was touched. 'So that's why you transferred Joe to another sector of the estate.'

'That's it.' Anstey poured tea and offered it, nodding at a plate of scones. 'My daily does those – they're good.'

'Well, thanks ... ' Henry couldn't resist home-made scones. He munched for a moment. 'If you're not in favour and Joe's not in favour, couldn't you persuade your directors not to disturb the path?'

'We have to make the best use of the land, Henry. After all, N.Y. Estates has to answer to its shareholders like every other company. How would you explain an asset left unproductive?'

'I see that.... It all comes of treating farming like a factory process!'

'I know, I know, you don't agree with that. But the kind of farming you approve of belongs in that museum you couldn't get started. If I may say so, that's a pointer – it's not commercially viable even as an educational scheme. No use hiding our heads in the sand – land can only be farmed these days with money enough to have machines and buildings of the right kind, and to do that you have to treat it like a business, with a profit and loss account and dividends for your stockholders.'

Henry sighed and let it go. He had had that quiet word that Annie recommended and learned from it that the footpath must go, despite the regrets of Richard Anstey. He couldn't see that he had done much good, except, perhaps, that he was no longer angry and indignant.

As he left Home Farm he understood what Annie had been trying to convey: that the mere idea of a 'protest meeting' implied entrenched antagonism. Was that what Tom Merrick had intended?

Pat Merrick had felt it only fair to tell Jackie and Sandie about their father's actions in organising the meeting. They would hear about it soon enough anyway. Sandie was impressed but puzzled. Jackie was proud. 'See,' he said, 'he's got a lot in him that folk don't give him credit for.'

As it was Sunday, Pat had chores to do. The youngsters decided to cadge a lift from the Longthorns and go into Hotten where they could see a few friends and spend an hour or two over a Coke. They were on their way back to meet the Longthorns in the parking lot when they heard themselves hailed by a familiar voice.

'What you two doing here?' their father inquired.

'Oh ... just mooching around,' Jackie said.

He fell into step with them. He had been out to fetch the Sunday papers, having been in bed until noon. 'Everything all right?' he asked.

'Yeh, not bad. Listen, Dad, that's a great thing about the footpath!'

'Oh aye. Not bad, is it, for an idea by your old Dad?'

'Think you're gonna stop 'em?'

'Course we are. Don't want you all walking through mud to get to the school bus, do we?' He described his plans for the forthcoming meeting then went on to ask if they'd be there.

'Dunno. Mum doesn't seem to want us to go, although we're involved more than most, aren't we?'

'Aye. Well, never mind, best do what your mum says. How's school?'

Both youngsters groaned inwardly at the same old question. Sandie said coolly that she was getting on well

114

and hoped to have no problems with O levels, might even stay on for A levels.

'That's the way!' Merrick said with enthusiasm. 'I've missed out through not having a proper education.'

'I wouldn't mind so much if it was a *proper* education,' Jackie groaned, 'but who cares about history and geography? I wanted to do woodwork and metalwork, but that stupid timetable wouldn't allow it.'

Sandie gave him a glance of sympathy. 'It's a fact they only push you in subjects where you stand to get a certificate.'

'But you could get a certificate for woodwork if you got your timetable right, eh?'

'Suppose so,' Jackie said morosely.

'Tell you what, lad,' Merrick suggested. 'What about if I had a word wi' your teachers? Put the point to them?'

Jackie looked doubtful.

'Not me alone,' Merrick went on at once, his thoughts racing ahead. 'I mean, me and your Mum. If we were to see t'headmaster?'

Jackie exchanged a look with his sister. She gave a faint shrug. 'Couldn't do any harm, I s'pose.'

'What do you think, Sandie?'

Sandie, flattered at being asked her opinion, said she thought visits by parents made a good impression. 'Taking an interest – they like that.'

'Okay then. You ask your Mum if she'll go wi' me. Think it over and ask her. After all, we both want what's best for you, don't we?' He gave Sandie a hug. 'Been nice to see you, love. You're getting to be a right little smasher. Got all the boys after you, eh?'

'Oh, Dad!' sighed Sandie in the accepted manner for parental opinions. But she was pleased.

'Your Mum and me were chatting ... Well, you don't want to hear that. Be nice if we could work things out, get a house and be together again, like.'

He paused, awaiting their reactions. They both looked wary. He knew he had said enough for the moment. 'Well, must get back, cook me own tea. See you again soon, I hope.' He waved and walked away.

Sandie and Jackie resumed their way towards the car park. 'She won't have him back,' Sandie said, stopping suddenly to face her brother.

He cocked his head to think. 'Would you like her to?' he asked.

Sandie began to walk on without replying.

'You reckon she'd rather have Jack Sugden?'

She paused until he caught up with her again. Then she shrugged.

'You got to think something!' Jackie cried, his voice angry. 'You can't just shrug about it!'

'It won't make any difference what we think,' she replied.

'Of course it will!'

'No, it won't. Mum will make up her own mind.'

'Meaning it doesn't matter what Dad wants?'

'It matters to *him*. But she doesn't take so much account of that as she did once.'

They walked on for a time side by side, the boy tall and almost a man, the girl small and fragile, still very much a child in body though mature in mind.

'What about if she knew we'd like them to go back together, though? I mean if we told her?'

She shrugged.

He felt the movement and was vexed with her. Why couldn't she see that their parents were making a mess of all their lives, and that they, the children, had to take a hand? 'I'm going to ask her,' he said. 'Right out – I'm going to ask her.'

Sandie made as if to speak, then shrugged. What was the use? If he wanted to make a fool of himself, why should she stop him?

His opportunity came that evening. Sandie went to see Jill Firkettle, who needed help with her algebra homework. Jackie, having worked himself up to it since four o'clock, set about talking to his mother.

When Sandie had gone out with her algebra exercise book, he offered to make a cup of coffee. It was so unusual that Pat was at once alert. He busied himself in

116

the little kitchen then brought the coffee to her where she sat opposite the television set.

'We met Dad this afternoon in Hotten,' he began.

'Jackie!'

'Oh, not on purpose. He just happened along. He was saying he'd like to go to the school and have a chat with them about me doing metalwork.'

His mother could find nothing to say. Tom, taking an interest in the children's schooling?

'He wants you to go with him, see Mr Spofforth, Mum.'

She said nothing. At least she understood now why this sudden enthusiasm for education.

'Why don't you get on with him, Mum?' Jackie asked.

She sighed. She shook her head and turned to look at the television screen.

Jackie got up and switched it off. 'He wants to come back and live with us again, Mum.'

'I know that, lad. He told me that.'

'Then why? Why don't we . . . ' He stopped, swallowed, then started again. 'I don't like seeing him pushed out.'

'He weren't pushed out!' she flashed. 'He went!'

'He didn't! You packed up and took us away –'

'He wasn't there, Jackie. You know that as well as I do. He'd gone off with his pals, to the racing. If I hadn't taken you and Sandie away, you'd have ended up in care, because he was doing nowt to support us.'

'But he wants to now! It'll be different!'

She shook her head. 'I'm not going back to him, Jackie. I can't go through all that again.'

'What? What's so wrong about him? Okay he drinks, but so do a lot of other folk's fathers – he's got faults, I know he has, but he's our Dad!'

How could she possibly explain to him? Explain that the mere idea of being touched by Tom Merrick filled her with revulsion, that his violent character put her in fear and not without cause, that she was exhausted from years of trying to cope with his fecklessness, his drunkenness, his unkindness . . .

'Is it because you want to marry Jack Sugden?'

117

Pat sat up and stared at her son. 'What ... what made you ask that?' And then, wearily, 'I suppose your father put it into your head.'

'No, he didn't.' Jackie's dark eyes flashed with anger. 'If you want to know, it's the talk of the village!'

Chapter Ten

The vicar of Beckindale had more experience of running a public meeting than most of his parishioners, and the more he thought of it the more it worried him that the protest meeting about the footpath should be left in the hands of Tom Merrick. Even taking the purely Christian view, that the man meant well, what did he know of asking for proposers and seconders and taking a vote?

Mr Hinton went to Emmerdale to see the man he thought best qualified to take it over. 'I think you ought to, Henry,' he urged. 'You're far more experienced.'

'But how can I? I didn't call the meeting. I'm just a member of the audience like everyone else.'

'That's not true and you know it. What do you think, Annie?'

'I agree with you, vicar, I've already had my say on that.'

'It's a bit difficult, Ma,' Jack put in. 'Henry can hardly walk up to Merrick and say, "Here, I'm going to take charge."'

'I wasn't suggesting he should do exactly that,' the vicar said with a faint smile.

'But you think I should gently take the reins out of his hands, is that it?'

'It could end up a right shouting match if Tom Merrick is the only one supposed to be keeping order,' Dolly said. She glanced at her husband. Matt looked uncomfortable at saying something critical and contented himself with nodding.

After some discussion it was agreed that Henry and

118

Jack should seek out Merrick and ask how he was going to run the affair. They would then make 'Suggestions' – an offer he couldn't refuse, as Matt quoted. Before setting off for Hotten in search of him, Henry had a moment alone in the Emmerdale kitchen which he used for an urgent phone call to his stockbroker.

They reached Hotten by lunchtime. Jack had no idea of Merrick's address but had realised he could get it from young Jackie, who was coming out of school for the lunch break. Surprised at being sought out by Jack, the lad looked embarrassed. 'What d'you want his address for?' he said with some pugnacity, thinking it had something to do with his mother.

'Mr Wilks and I want to have a chat about whether he needs any help over this meeting he's running,' Jack said.

'Oh.' It hardly seemed possible to refuse the information on those grounds, so Jackie gave it. He stood looking after the Land-Rover as it drove away.

'That were Jack Sugden, weren't it?' one of his pals remarked. 'The feller that's gonna be your step-dad, eh?'

'Oh, drop dead,' Jackie replied.

Merrick was not in the least pleased to see Henry and Jack. He had been just about to set out for his lunchtime session at the local. His face darkened in suspicion. 'What d'you want?' he demanded.

Henry took it upon himself to be the diplomat. He explained their anxiety, asked Merrick if he'd got out an agenda, and whether he was going to have it duplicated or read it out. Blinded by the glitter of this know-how, Merrick had to admit he hadn't got that far. In fact, he hadn't even thought of it.

'Well, if you'll rough something out, I'll get it typed up for you, and I'm sure the vicar will let us use the photo-copier –'

'Oh, him,' grunted Merrick. 'He doesn't want any part of it.'

'But he won't refuse the use of the photo-copier – it was

119

bought out of public funds for parish announcements and so on.'

'Well, all right then. Half a mo.' Merrick sat down at the table littered with empty cups and milk cartons, found a piece of paper, and wrote out a few ideas. One, announcement of purpose. Two, introduction of platform speakers. Here he paused. Who was going to do the actual speaking about the iniquities of the footpath? 'Er ... I suppose you wouldn't take on the job of putting the case against it, Mr Wilks?'

Henry, of course, would. And suggested Jack should second his proposal that the destruction of the footpath should be resisted. Merrick made no demur. He didn't care who spoke or what occurred: all he wanted was to be shown to have taken up the cause when no one else would make the move.

As they drove back to Beckindale, Henry said softly: 'I wonder what he's really up to?'

'You don't think he's a reformed character trying to help the community?'

'He hadn't a thought in his head beyond sitting on that platform looking noble. Doing any actual work ... he'd not thought of it.'

They stopped off at the Woolpack for a drink before going home. Joe was there, listening to Amos's lament that, because Mr Wilks was 'on holiday' at Emmerdale, he had no one to stand in for him in the bar. 'I shan't be able to be at the meeting to report it,' he groaned. 'An important local event and I shan't be there!' He looked hopefully at Henry as he said the last few words, raising his voice so he could be heard.

'Sorry, Amos,' Henry said. 'But I've got to be there. I'm going to be one of the platform party.'

'Thank heaven for that,' Joe said. 'I began to think it was all in Merrick's hands – and that could have been a disaster.'

'You going to be there, Joe?' Jack inquired, taking the pint Amos had drawn for him.

His brother hesitated. 'I don't know about that. Got our jobs to think of, haven't we?'

'You what?'

'Seth and me ... No matter how we feel about t'footpath, it wouldn't look too good if we supported the opposition, would it.'

'Well,' said Jack, 'That's an angle I hadn't really thought of ... '

'Aye, think on, Jack,' said Joe. 'How many in Beckindale will feel their jobs are threatened if they protest against N.Y. Estates ploughing up a footpath?'

That evening, as they worked in the mistle, Henry was fetching the measures of feed when he paused suddenly. 'Hey.'

'For horses,' Matt said, in automatic response dredged up from his childhood. 'Watch, Henry – you're tipping the pan.'

Henry righted it. 'What Joe was saying about jobs today, Jack.'

'Aye?' Jack said, fitting the liner against the cow's udder.

'You know we've said to each other as it was funny that Anstey made such a mess of this ploughing-up business. I mean, we could see it would have made more sense to do it as quickly as possible before we could all start objecting.'

'Aye, it's puzzled me,' Matt agreed.

'Seth let the cat out of the bag,' Jack put in. 'He mentioned it to Jackie, who told Pat.'

'You what?' said Henry, twirling so that the feed in the pan went over the edge. He stopped, set down the dish, and put his fists on his hips. 'Well, the crafty double-dealing old tyke ... '

'Who, Seth? You're right, of course, but what brought that on?'

'He told Jackie. He told me! D'you know what I think? I think that tricky old fox has been going round dropping hints here and there because he wanted someone to do something about the footpath but dared not do it himself – because of offending N.Y. Estates!'

'And Amos knew,' Jack added. 'Somebody had alerted him.'

'What d'you bet it was Seth?'

'Well, then, what he's done,' Matt said, 'was to get us all ready to fight it – he didn't want to see a traditional footpath –'

'Do you mind?' Jack interrupted. 'Seth didn't do it out of noble principles. Lower Puddle Path is his shortcut to his pheasant coops.'

They paused in their work, looking at one another. 'What it comes to is this,' Henry said. 'We're having this protest meeting, and it's all been arranged for us somehow by two chaps we don't think too strong on the love-thy-neighbour angle.'

'We're being used,' Jack said. 'That's what it is.'

'But that doesn't matter, does it,' said Matt. 'Fact is, we don't want the footpath to go.'

'Aye, but we've got to put up a proper case because quite a lot of folk aren't going to support us in public. They don't want to endanger their jobs, I quite see their point. And Tom Merrick's not too convincing, is he? He doesn't even live in Beckindale.'

'No, but Pat does . . . '

'Aye,' Jack said. It occurred to him it might be a good idea to get Pat to come to the meeting and say a few words from the floor about the difficulties and anxieties of getting back and forth to the caravan if the footpath were gone. He decided he'd go and see her next morning. He couldn't go tonight, he'd promised to stay in and keep Ma company while the others went to a film in Hotten.

But next morning Pat Merrick had a visitor before Jack could finish his chores and get there. Her husband was waiting outside the caravan at around half-past eight, in the shadows of the far hedgerow, watching for Jackie and Sandie to leave for the school bus.

When they had gone, he crossed the field and opened the door without knocking. He stepped inside. Pat, clearing up to get ready for work, turned in astonishment.

He advanced until he was towering over her. He held out a manila envelope, crushed in his fist. 'What's this?'

he snarled. 'I got it this morning. What's this about a divorce?'

She backed away from him. She had seen him like this before with that red look in his eyes.

'You never told me! When I asked you to take me back, you just sat there and let me say it all and you never told me you'd started this!'

'No ... I ... wanted you to get the official papers, to see I really mean it, Tom.'

'Mean it? It may be what you mean but it's not what I mean, you deceitful little bitch! I'm not having any divorce!'

'It's not up to you to say. I've made the application –'

'And you're going to cancel it.'

'No, Tom, I'm not –'

'Don't be so stupid and selfish! I don't want a divorce and neither do the kids! They want us to get back together again – you ask 'em.'

'I don't have to ask. Jackie told me. But Jackie doesn't have to ...' She let the words tail off. She might have said, He doesn't have to share his bed with you, he doesn't have to endure your so-called affection.

'He doesn't have to what?'

'He doesn't have to face you when you're like this, ready to take your fist to me.'

He made a great effort and got control of himself. 'Listen, Pat,' he said, using the arguments he'd rehearsed all the way to Beckindale from Hotten, 'I may not have done the best by you in the past, but that's all over now. I told you afore, I've learned my lesson. I'll make a new start and be responsible – No, don't shake your head, I'll do it. For the sake of the kids, Pat.'

'The kids are almost grown-up,' she said. 'In a couple of years they'll have left home, probably.' And then I'd be left with only you, was the unspoken end to her comment.

'They won't leave if we're together,' he urged. 'I'll get a job, find a house –'

'I've heard it all before, Tom! I can't go through it all

123

again. I've had enough . . . at the end of the road . . . I'm going through with the divorce.'

'No, listen.' He came to her, took both her hands. 'Doesn't it mean anything to you that I love you? I do, honest I do! I'll do anything, if you'll drop this!' He swept the envelope off the table onto the floor. 'We can make a new life together. Everything'll be different—'

'I've heard it all before, Tom,' she interrupted, her voice breaking.

'But I mean it this time, I really mean it! You've got what you wanted wi' those papers, you've thrown a real scare into me. We'll start again—'

'For the hundredth time?' And now some anger had given her strength. 'You've said it all before and where's it got me? Here!' Her gesture took in the cramped caravan, the empty field outside. 'This is what I've got from listening to you in the past. Living on Mr Anstey's goodwill, on Social Security and a rotten part-time job . . . I've had enough, Tom. It's over.'

For answer he tried to put his arms round her, to show her by physical warmth what his words seemed to lack. 'Don't do that!' she cried, struggling in his grasp.

'I just want you to listen—'

'And I don't want to hear!'

'Let's kiss and make up,' he went on, disregarding her efforts to get away. 'I love you, Pat.'

She put her fists against his chest. 'The only person you've ever loved is yourself!'

'No, no, it's you. I've never cared for any other lass—'

'Don't tell lies, Tom, d'you think I don't know about all that?'

'If it's that you're upset about —'

'Oh, don't you understand? That's nothing – I don't bother about it – I just want – I just want to have my life to myself—'

'Oh, that's rubbish. Come on, love, just a kiss.' He held her so close she couldn't struggle. Seeing no help for it, she let him kiss her. But her body was rigid, her face like stone. He let her go, leaned back, and frowned. 'I see. Like that, is it.'

She tried to get away but he caught her wrist. 'I don't need to ask who you'd rather have kissing you. Jack Sugden. You want your old flame back, is that it? Eh? Eh?'

She hunched her shoulders as if to protect herself from his searching glance. He held her wrist in a grasp like a vice.

'I got eyes, you know,' he whispered, his voice thick with jealousy. 'I've seen you and him. Stuck-up, self-satisfied bastard! You want to get rid of me so you can wed him, that's it, isn't it?' Suddenly he shook her ferociously. 'Isn't it? Isn't it?'

'No, Tom – you're wrong – don't, you're hurting me!'

'I mean to hurt you!' he ground out. 'You've been asking for it, lass! You're not going to any Sugden!'

'You're talking nonsense – '

'You're my wife and that's the way it's going to stay –'

'Tom, please! Please! You'll break my wrist!'

'I'll break more'n that. You say you're taking back them papers –'

He was bending back her arm so that she had to grovel on her knees. He was glaring down at her. 'You're hurting me, Tom –!'

'Say you'll cancel it. Say it!'

Blinded by tears of pain and fear, she shook her head. And through the mist she saw his fist descending on her, for the first of many blows.

Chapter Eleven

Jack arrived to find the door of the caravan banging to and fro in the blustery March wind. He got out of the Land-Rover, frowning a little, wondering if Pat had gone out without securing it properly. As he crossed the cinder path he heard the sound of sobbing. He leapt the steps to the caravan's interior and hurtled in.

Pat was lying on the floor with her face hidden in the seat of a chair and her arms round her head.

'Pat!' He stooped over her, trying to raise her. She cowered away from him. 'Pat, it's me, Jack! What's happened?'

She said something in a muffled voice.

'What? Let me look at you, love. What happened?' He put both hands on her head and tilted it up. Her face came into view. The swollen red patches on her cheeks glared up at him, heightened by the scarlet of blood from a split lip.

'My God!' He knelt beside her. He took out his handkerchief to dab gently at the bloodied lip. She winced, and he stopped at once. 'Who did this?' he demanded.

'It was Tom.' She took the handkerchief from him and mopped at her eyes, wincing as she touched the swollen places.

'But in heaven's name, why? Was he drunk?'

'He got a letter from my lawyer today. It was about a divorce.'

'Oh, I see.' He put an arm about her and helped her up. She was trembling with reaction, still shuddering from sobs. 'Look, love, you must see a doctor –'

'No, no, I can't –'

'You've got to. Come on now, I've got the Land-Rover outside.'

'No, Jack, I don't want anyone – '

'You need that cut seen to. I'll take you to the hospital.' He found her coat and draped it over her shoulders with one hand while with the other he guided her to the door. 'You ought to see the police too.'

'No, don't say that – it's bad enough –'

'Mind the steps.' He helped her down. He was intent on what he was doing so that he didn't see Seth Armstrong on the footpath, en route to Swinney Copse to see his pheasant enclosure.

126

'He can't get away with this, Pat. You've got to lay charges—'

'No, don't you see? He got a suspended sentence before. If I bring him to court over this, he'll go to prison—'

'That's his lookout, Pat! He's asked for it!' He was shepherding her across the forecourt to his Land-Rover, turned away from Seth, who stood quite still, unashamedly listening.

'But the kids, Jack! They'd never forgive me if I landed their father in jail!'

Jack paused with his hand on the handle of the Land-Rover. 'Come on now, get in.'

'But promise you won't—'

'We'll talk about it on the way. Are you all right?' He had put her in the passenger seat.

'Aye, I'm all right — Jack, my handbag—'

'I'll get it.' He ran back to fetch it while she sat with eyes closed. She heard the slam of the caravan's door then next moment they were in motion, Jack trying to move gently over the grassy surface of Upper Puddle Meadow to the field gate leading out to Ridge Lane.

At the hospital a blue-clad sister took charge of Pat immediately and led her away after a frosty glance at Jack. He waited with anxiety for about twenty minutes, at the end of which time a young woman doctor came out in a white coat.

'Well,' she remarked, 'she says she stumbled and fell face first against the dresser, but if you think I'm going to believe that, you've another think coming.'

'She asked me to—'

'I'm trying to get her to call the police and I hope she will. I warn you—'

'Excuse me—'

'My report to the magistrate will be very detailed, Mr Merrick!'

'That's what I'm trying to tell you,' Jack got in at last. 'I'm not the husband, I'm a friend.'

'Oh,' said the doctor, and had the grace to look ashamed. 'I'm sorry, but it makes me so wild! These women come here with bruises all over them and declare they walked into a door. I don't know why they refuse to press charges.'

'It baffles me too.'

'Of course, if there are children, that always weighs heavily. For some reason these brutal husbands seem to manage to be very appealing to their children, I don't know how.'

Jack sighed. 'Well, what's happening now? Can I take her home?'

'We've given her some painkillers and sent her for an X-ray –'

'An X-ray?' Jack said in alarm.

'Just a precaution. She has a bad bruise above the hairline which actually might have been caused by falling against the dresser – I just want to make sure there's no serious damage.'

'How long will she be?'

'About half an hour. She's very anxious that someone should tell her employers she can't come in.'

'I'll do that,' Jack said. 'They're not far off – I'll be back in ten minutes.'

Mrs Miles of the Market Cafe was in a great state of indignation when Jack went in. He gave Pat's apologies and received a snort of annoyance. 'About time she let us know! Snowed under, we are, no one to clear the tables and everybody in here for coffee and early lunch –'

'She's had a bit of an accident –'

'Serious? No? Then she could at least have got to a phone. It's most inconsiderate –'

'She's in hospital at this moment having an X-ray,' Jack cut in sharply.

'Oh?'

'Suspected concussion. So it'll be a day or two before she's back.'

'Oh ... well ... in that case ... '

Jack turned on his heel and marched out. Not a word of sympathy. Pat's job certainly wasn't much help to her in finding the world a good place to live in.

When he took her home she seemed very drowsy. No

doubt the painkillers had that effect. He made her promise to lie down for a couple of hours and privately determined to ask his mother to come over with something for the evening meal. As he was going she fished out the handkerchief he had lent her to hold against her split lip. 'I'm sorry it's in such a mess,' she apologised. 'I'd say I'd wash and iron it, but your Ma can probably do it better in her washing machine.'

'That's all right, love.' He gave her a kiss on the top of her head and left her.

Everyone at Emmerdale must be wondering what on earth had happened to him. Well, they'd have to wonder a while longer because he decided to drop in on the vicar, enlist his help for Pat. He left the Land-Rover in the verge near the village green rather than take it up the steeply banked lane that led to the vicarage.

Thus it was that Merrick, slouching through Emmerdale on his way to the Maltshovel, saw the Emmerdale Land-Rover standing unattended. He recognised it; it was still recognisably new and shiny. He walked alongside it and looked in, out of envious curiosity more than anything else.

On the seat was a crumpled and bloodstained handkerchief. He reached in and picked it up. It was embroidered in the corner, white on white, Jack's initials done by Annie for a Christmas present. With no formed plan, simply out of covetousness and mischief, he pocketed it.

At the Maltshovel he nodded to one or two acquaintances. Merrick preferred the Maltshovel to the Woolpack – it had a jukebox and served substantial snacks. He ordered a pint and a helping of shepherd's pie. His old friend Whippy Barton waved at him as he turned from the counter. Merrick joined him at the table.

The truth was, Merrick needed company. The memory of what he'd done was haunting him. He knew, past all argument, that he had put an end to his marriage once and for all. Perhaps he'd never had much hopes of getting Pat to live with him again, but he had always thought he would have a hold on her. Now she really intended to divorce him. Nothing he could ever say now would persuade her to change her mind. And once the kids saw that face of hers, it would be goodbye to seeing much of them: he wouldn't be able to use them as a lever against her.

It was all Jack Sugden's fault. He put her up to it, you could bet a million on it.

'Well, how's things, Tom?' Whippy inquired. Whippy was so called because he was little and half-starved like a whippet.

'Rotten. What you doing in Beckindale?'

'Not much, and that's a fact. Lost a packet at Doncaster last week – I'm trying to live quiet and economise.'

'Huh,' grunted Merrick, and went for a refill. When he came back Whippy eyed him with curiosity.

'How's the missus?'

'How'd I know?' Merrick sneered. 'Got no time for me any more. It's all Jack Sugden this, Jack Sugden that.'

'Aye, I heard summat,' Whippy agreed.

'What? What did you hear?'

'Only that they was friendly,' the little man said, edging away from the glare of anger.

'They're more than just friendly,' Merrick said. All at once his fertile brain had found a use for the handkerchief. He fished it out of his pocket and flourished it. 'See this? Got his initial on it, hasn't it?' He pulled out the corner so that it was visible. There it was, in fine Italian capitals: J.S. 'And where do you think I found that?'

'Go on, tell us,' urged Whippy.

'In the caravan where she's living. And not in the living room, mind you.'

'You what?' said Whippy. He grinned. 'Like that, is it?'

'But it's all right,' Merrick said in a mincing tone. 'Cos they're going to get married, you see.' He nodded at those listening.

'Is that a fact?' Whippy said.

'Well, remains to be seen, don't it? But that's what she thinks. But we know what Jack Sugden's like, don't we lads?'

The men in the bar-room nodded and nudged each other. Jack Sugden, oh aye, hot stuff, Italian film stars in

his place in Rome, pictures of him in the *Sunday Gazette*
... And now Pat Merrick ...

Jack himself was meanwhile with Mr Hinton. 'She's
been very badly knocked about,' he told the vicar. 'Yet
she refuses to go to the police ... '

'I'll go and see her later this afternoon. She needs to
rest for the moment, I imagine.' Hinton was deeply
concerned. Although Pat wasn't a churchgoer, he regarded her as one of his flock, the more so as her children
had still to make their start in life and needed guidance.

'Try to persuade her to see Ted Edwards,' Jack said.

Hinton shook his head.

'You won't?'

'It's not my place to urge any course of action on Mrs
Merrick, and certainly not to ask her to take any kind of
vengeance, Jack. You may not put much trust in it, but I
still think there's a chance that Tom Merrick will turn over
a new leaf.'

'If I may say so, Donald, that's the triumph of optimism
over experience.'

'What else is Christianity?' the vicar said with a weary
smile.

When Jack got home the entire family were in the
kitchen. The midday meal was over. It had been eaten to
a continual chorus of 'Where can Jack have got to?'

When he told them of the morning's events, they were
shocked. Even Matt said in a sad tone: 'He's a bad lot,
Tom Merrick, no two ways about it.'

'There's no doubt he really did beat her up?' Henry
said. 'I mean – he didn't just push her and she fell against
something?'

Jack gave him a look.

'No, I see it was deliberate ... This is dreadful.'

'I'll tell you one thing. I'm not appearing on any public
platform with that man, and you can take that as final.'

Henry put his hands in his pockets and surveyed the
fireplace for a moment. 'Well now ... '

'Now look here, Henry! The man's a blackguard – '

'It seems so, lad. Yet that meeting's still as important
as it ever was.'

'I'm convinced now that he only got it up for his own glorification.'

'All the more reason why we shouldn't just back out and let him have things all his own way.'

'Henry's right, Jack,' said his mother.

'I can't be in conversation with the man,' Jack said. 'If I speak to him I'll hit him!'

'You mean you'll come down to his level?' inquired Matt.

'It's the only level he seems to understand –'

'There you are. You keep saying it. He's not the man to be running a meeting of that kind –'

'I wish it had never been suggested.'

'You mean you think we should just let the footpath go? Because if we do, it'll only be one more hardship Pat Merrick has to put up with.'

'Oh, Lord,' Jack groaned.

'Look, you don't have to speak to him, Jack. You only have to turn up and play your part on the platform.'

The argument went on for almost half an hour. It only ended when duties elsewhere called them away. But after thinking it over Jack had to agree that Henry was right. The meeting should be supervised by people who had the best interests of the village at heart, not by Tom Merrick.

Annie took it in her stride on being asked to drop in on Pat but Dolly vetoed it. 'That's a long walk. I'll go. I'll take a casserole, eh?'

She found Jackie and Sandie getting the evening meal. She produced the casserole, explaining that it was to save Pat the chore of cooking. 'How is she?' she inquired.

'Dunno. She's in bed, told us to see to ourselves.' Jackie frowned at Dolly. 'How did you know she wouldn't be up to cook for us?'

'She didn't tell you she had to go to hospital to have stitches in her lip?'

'What?' both youngsters cried in chorus.

Sandie turned as if to go into the bedroom. Dolly caught her by the elbow. 'No, Sandie, leave her alone. She's had enough for today.'

'But . . . what happened? How did it –?'

'Your mother says she fell and hit her face. That was this morning, soon after you left for school.'

'Oh, that's awful. To think of her lying here all alone –'

'It wasn't for long. Our Jack came by and took her to hospital.'

'Jack Sugden?' Jackie said in a suddenly hostile voice.

Dolly looked at him. 'Your father wasn't here to look after her. Somebody had to do it.'

'Yeh . . . well . . . '

'Tell her to look after herself. Come over to the farm if you want anything.'

'Thank you, we'll manage,' Jackie said stiffly.

'I'll bring back the dish,' Sandie said with a smile that tried to make amends for her brother's coldness.

When Dolly had gone, Jackie shoved the casserole aside. 'Nosy lot! Why can't they leave us alone!'

'She's only trying to be kind, Jackie –'

'She only came to find out what she could. I bet she's going around saying it was Dad that gave Mum that cut lip! Well, I'm not having it!'

'Nobody's saying anything, Jackie. Don't always be so ready to take offence –'

'Oh, girls are all the same,' Jackie said in disgust. 'Never want to stand up for themselves.'

Sandie said no more. She had thoughts of her own, one of which was that Dolly Skilbeck had known more than she reported and whatever it was, it was serious. Sandie had seen her mother with bruises before, bruises caused by falling over and knocking against something. Sandie had never believed it then and she didn't believe it now.

Pat's appearance improved a little each day. But she stayed at home, half out of fear of running across Tom and half out of shame. Her husband had no such inhibitions. He was out and about in Beckindale, acting out his part as champion of a just cause.

Amos had unexpectedly found a helper willing to take on the bar at the Woolpack on the evening of the meeting.

It was none other than Seth Armstrong. 'I don't mind lending a hand, Amos. In fact, I think it might be very enjoyable,' the gamekeeper said, with visions of an unlimited succession of free drinks before him.

'Nay, Seth, it needs a lot of character, a lot of tact.'

'Well, I've got character, and as to tact, customers of t'Woolpack have got along wi'out it for a good many years now.'

'What d'you mean, got along without it? Let me tell you, if it weren't for my handling of many a tricky situation, there'd have been trouble here.'

'I think I can handle any tricky situations that might arise, Amos.'

'Nay, but it's not summat I can decide on just in a minute –'

'Well, if you think you could get somebody else, you go ahead, lad. But t'way I hear it, most of t'village is going to t'meeting.'

'Aye,' said Amos, thinking about that. If there were few customers, how could Seth go far wrong? Surely even Seth Armstrong could pull half a dozen pints without getting in a muddle. And Amos really must get to the meeting. It was an event of great importance which the *Courier* was interested in – they'd send another man if he himself couldn't go. And that he couldn't have borne.

So at last on the Saturday morning he reluctantly agreed to accept Seth's offer of help. There were only a few hours to go before the meeting.

Josh Potter, the verger, was worried too. No one had been in touch with him about the practical details of that evening's meeting. How many chairs was he supposed to set out? Was there to be a table on the stage, or not? If so, was it to be in front of the stage curtains or were the curtains to be left open and the platform party actually to sit on stage?

Perplexed about these points, he had written to Tom Merrick and also gone to see Mr Hinton. The result was that Merrick arrived outside the hall at about mid-afternoon, at the same time as the vicar who had summoned Henry and Jack.

'Afternoon,' Merrick said with polite joviality. 'Seems we all had the same idea, eh? Get the place ready for the evening?'

'I was a little perturbed,' said the vicar. 'Nothing seemed to have been arranged –'

'I'm sorry, I should have been in touch,' Merrick apologised. He hadn't in fact given the meeting much thought, had no idea anyone had to take charge of such mundane activities as putting out chairs.

'We'll go in, shall we, and decide how we're going to arrange things?' Henry said.

'Righto, lead the way.'

'Er ... You have the key, presumably,' said the vicar.

Merrick looked blank. He gazed around, and met Jack Sugden's contemptuous gaze. He coloured up. 'Nay, vicar, I thought you'd have it?'

Jack, addressing no one in particular, remarked: 'That's odd, since the vicar isn't even supposed to be here.'

Merrick frowned angrily but controlled his temper. 'I'll go and get the key from Potter,' he volunteered.

'That would be a good idea.'

They waited around until he came back, pink with vexation and haste. 'Potter's out. Neighbour says he's taken his wife into Hotten for a morning's shopping.'

'Very efficiently organised,' Jack remarked to the hall door.

'You mean we can't get in until he gets back?' Henry inquired.

'Seems so.'

Henry glanced at his watch. 'Well, it's twelve-fifteen now. 'Fraid I can't hang about until Potter gets back – I promised to take Annie out for a walk.'

'And I, too, have other duties,' said Mr Hinton. 'In any case, I don't wish to interfere ... '

'I'll see to it,' Merrick said, glowering at being shown up. 'I don't mind doing it all on my own.'

'Jack, you can pop in and lend him a hand, can't you?' Hinton urged.

'I've milking to do – '

'I'll be back by then and Matt and I can do it, Jack,'

Henry assured him. His nod and smile said: Remember, it's all for the good of the cause.

Jack seriously doubted if he could be in Merrick's company alone without having a flaming row. But he recalled that Potter would be at the hall too, and he merely shrugged and agreed.

Tom Merrick was furious with everyone for this display of his own inefficiency. He was particularly furious with Jack Sugden, who said such high-and-mighty things to nobody in particular and was clearly getting at him. In a state of suppressed rage Merrick took himself off to the home of Whippy Barton, where he passed the time watching Saturday afternoon sport on the television until the pubs opened. He then took Whippy for a drink, and with the beer came inspiration.

'Here,' he whispered to his friend, 'want to earn a tenner?'

'Who doesn't?' Whippy said, wiping froth from his mouth.

'Here you are then.' Merrick slipped a note from his pocket and passed it to Whippy.

'What's it for, though?'

'A little job like you done for that mate of yours that went bankrupt – remember? Him with the hardware shop.'

'Oh, you mean Toby Yalethorpe? That needed the insurance?'

'Aye, a quick ten minutes work wi' a box o' matches, Whippy.'

'Right, you're on,' said Whippy.

At about five o'clock Merrick went to fetch the key from Josh Potter. He didn't expect to see Jack Sugden at the hall: he had seen the dislike in the other man's eyes and understood Jack's wish to stay away from him. But, in fact, Jack had been given a lecture by Henry which, though it didn't improve his opinion of Merrick, had made him feel he ought not to show open contempt. 'Pat Merrick doesn't want it known that he knocked her about, Jack. It's up to you not to change your manner towards him in public otherwise everybody'll guess.'

'I just wish they would. I wish the constable could get to hear of it and take steps.'

'Nay, Pat doesn't want that. She's thinking of her son and daughter, lad. How can it help matters if you make an enemy of their father?'

So, greatly to Merrick's surprise, Jack was at the hall. Josh Potter, who was expected home for his tea, left them to it. They were hard at work in almost total silence putting chairs in rows when the sound of a fire engine could be heard on the road over the bridge.

'Hey-up,' said Merrick, raising his head. 'Trouble?'

Jack shrugged and finished straightening the last row. Then he pushed the table on stage and set two chairs behind it. 'How do you want this to go this evening?'

'I thought Mr Wilks could speak first, explaining the programme, and then you could speak about the loss it would be if the footpath was demolished.'

'Don't you want to speak first?'

'Nay, I'm not much of a hand with words.'

No, only with your fists, thought Jack. But he accepted Merrick's plan, set water jug, pencil and paper on the table, and left Merrick to lock up.

When he got home to Emmerdale he found his brother there. 'You heard?' Joe said. 'Two of our barns have gone up in flames. Value's about fifty thousand pounds.'

'Good God!' Jack exclaimed, startled. 'I heard the fire engine ... I'd no idea where it was going, though.' He eyed Joe. 'You look angry?'

'The fire chief said he was almost sure the fire was deliberate, Jack.'

'What? Oh no!' Jack threw himself onto a chair, gazing round the kitchen. 'That's all we need! If some nutcase who supports our case against N.Y. Estates has taken matters into his own hands, it'll look bad for us.'

'Anstey thinks it was someone with a grudge. And of course there are plenty of those around,' Joe said.

'He really thinks it was arson?'

'The police seem fairly sure.'

Annie sighed. 'Why is it that there's always someone

137

ready to do an act of malice like that? I hope it's cleared up soon because it spreads anxiety and suspicion . . . '

'Aye,' Matt agreed. 'Trouble is, all you find at a fire is charred wreckage. Difficult to know who did it.'

The evening meal was eaten in some gloom. They were all worried about the fire-raiser. Henry and Jack were nervous about the forthcoming meeting. Joe was depressed at the loss of two barns and their contents. There was very little conversation, even between Matt and Dolly, who seemed to have caught the general infection.

They left for the meeting in separate groups, Jack and Henry in Henry's car, Matt and Dolly in the Land-Rover. Joe had elected to stay at home to keep his mother company since Annie had said she didn't want to be present at an event which might end in acrimony.

Dolly was quiet as they drove. Matt said, 'Anything wrong, love?'

'I was just thinking, Matt. You heard the talk in the village – about Jack marrying Pat Merrick?'

'How can he, love? She's a married woman!'

'June Fairchild said her husband told her that Tom Merrick was in the Maltshovel t'other day, saying Pat had started divorce proceedings so she could wed Jack.'

'Oh, him.'

'But Jack does see a lot of her, Matt.'

'There's nowt in that, Dolly. They used to know each other years ago. I told you all about that. Of course he sees her. She needs friends.'

'But if they did get wed . . . ?'

'What if they did?'

'What would happen to us, Matt?'

He turned his head to look at her. 'What d'you mean? How would it affect us?'

'It'd be bound to. It would mean another person in the house, plus her two youngsters. Where would we put them all, Matt?'

Matt had returned his attention to his driving. 'Talk about supping sorrow with a long spoon,' he murmured. 'Come on, love, stop giving yourself the jitters about nowt.'

Dolly said no more. But she couldn't put the thought out of her mind. It might happen, one day. And if it did ..

The hall was packed. A murmurous sound rose from the audience. On the platform sat Jack, Henry and, between them, Tom Merrick. He rose in a deprecating way and knocked on the table with his fist.

'Well ... Fellow-villagers ... I'm not a talker. I want to leave the speechmaking to them as knows how to do it. I'll only say we've been waiting in hopes Mr Anstey would attend, but seems like he's got problems at the moment so I just say, to open the meeting here's Mr Wilks.'

Henry got up. There was an attentive silence. He looked over his audience and began briskly.

'Mr Anstey was to come and explain exactly what his company intended over Lower Puddle Path. I can only think the fire at Ridge Farm has delayed him. I hope he turns up because any decision we make here tonight depends on the attitude of N.Y. Estates. However, there's no doubt there is a clear intention to plough up the footpath, and I'm sure you agree with me that that's an infringement of the right of the public to –'

He broke off as a slight hubbub at the back of the hall caused heads to turn. Richard Anstey came in, flanked by two policemen in uniform. One of them was Ted Edwards, the village constable. The other was Sergeant MacArthur from Hotten. He detached himself from the trio and came to the edge of the platform.

'Mr Jack Sugden?' he inquired, addressing Jack.

'Yes.'

'I have to ask you to come with me to Hotten Police Station.'

Jack stared at him. A sibilant whisper of shock went round the hall. 'What on earth for?' Jack demanded.

'We need you to help in our inquiries with regard to the fire at Ridge Farm this afternoon.'

Chapter Twelve

It isn't exactly pleasant to be put into a police car and driven away in front of all your friends.

'Am I under arrest?' Jack asked.

'Of course not, Mr Sugden. We merely wish to ask you some questions.'

'Couldn't you have asked me at the hall?'

'This is a serious matter, sir. We want to talk about it in peace.'

Nothing more was said until they reached Hotten Police Station. There Jack was put into an interview room and left for a few minutes. Standard practice, he told himself. Time enough for the guilty to get nervous.

By and by Sergeant MacArthur came back. 'Now, Mr Sugden. Where were you at about five o'clock this afternoon?'

'At the village hall getting it ready for the meeting.'

'Indeed? Can anyone verify that statement?'

'I should imagine so. Dozens of folk must have seen me go in. And I was working with Tom Merrick.'

'I see. How long did you remain there?'

'Until about a quarter to six.'

'You were in each other's company all the time?'

'Yes.'

There was a pause. Sergeant MacArthur opened a folder he had before him and from it took a clear plastic bag. He pushed it forward towards Jack. 'Is that your handkerchief, Mr Sugden?'

Jack looked at it. It was roughly folded in four and smeared with blood, also stained with smoke and some singeing.

'May I take it out?'

'Of course.'

He did so, to reveal his intials in the corner. 'Yes, that's mine.'

'Can you explain how it came to be on the scene of the fire at Ridge Farm?'

Jack's mouth opened in a gasp of astonishment. 'No I can not!' He thought for a moment then said: 'The last time I remember seeing it was a few days ago. A friend of mine had some cuts and bruises to the face so I lent my handkerchief and took her to Hotten Hospital – '

'Her? Who?'

'I'd rather not say unless it becomes absolutely necessary. All I want to tell you is that she had my handkerchief on that day. She gave it back to me when I took her home. After that I don't remember seeing it again.'

'Hm ... Can anyone corroborate that it went missing?'

'No ... Yes! My mother can. Every day she collects up dirty clothes for laundering. She always collects shirt, handkerchief and socks from all of us. I remember her asking me what I'd done with my hankie.'

'Are you sure it was this one?'

'Certain. She mentioned it was one of those she'd embroidered that had gone missing. She did six of them for Christmas – she mentioned I'd only have five left by Easter and probably none by Whitsun.'

'I see, sir.' Sergeant MacArthur got up, gathering up his evidence. 'I'll ask you just to wait here, Mr Sugden.

He went to the CID room to report the conversation. 'Says he lost the handkerchief, and it sounds true enough – he can corroborate the point. He's got an alibi for the relevant time – he was with Tom Merrick.'

'Oh, Merrick,' said the CID inspector, as if to indicate what he thought of an alibi verified by such as he. Then he said: 'Hang on! Isn't there some gossip about Merrick's wife and this chap ... Jack Sugden? Wasn't it in the Sundays?'

'Right.'

'Ah,' said the CID man. And then, 'But Merrick has an alibi.'

'Yes. He was with Jack Sugden.'

'All the same ... pick him up, Jim.'

'Righto.'

Sergeant MacArthur went back to the interview room. 'I'll just get that typed up for you to sign, sir, and then you can go.'

'You're not sending me to Alcatraz then?'

Sergeant MacArthur had no sense of humour. 'If you'll just wait a few minutes, sir, the statement will be ready.' He gave a nod and went out, this time to get into the police car and set off yet again for Beckindale.

The meeting had broken up when he got there. The sudden removal of Jack Sugden had put a decided kink in the proceedings, particularly as Henry Wilks had excused himself to hurry in the wake of the police car. Anstey, remaining in the hall to play his part, had answered questions about the proposed use of Upper Puddle Field while Merrick sat by, looking smug. Without any clear decision the audience had dispersed.

Merrick was in the Maltshovel when MacArthur ran him to earth. 'I want a word with you, Merrick. Come with me.'

'What's this about, sergeant?' Merrick said in annoyance.

'Come along now, don't be troublesome.'

'I don't have to come. I haven't done anything.'

'I could always take you in on a charge of obstructing the police –'

'All right, all right. But this is a liberty!'

He remained silent until they were in the interview room. Then to his dismay a CID sergeant came in. 'Well, well, look who's here. We meet again, Tom.'

'Now look here, Mr Gunter, I haven't done owt ... '

'We'll see, we'll see. Where were you at about five o'clock this afternoon?'

'At Beckindale Parish Hall, getting it ready for the meeting.'

'Who was with you?'

'Nobody.'

'No? I thought you had a helper?'

'Nope, I done it all by myself.'

'That's funny, for Jack Sugden says he was with you.'

'No he wasn't.'

'You were on your own?'

'Yes.'

'That's a pity, Tom, because you're known to have a grudge against N.Y. Estates, so naturally you're one of the first people we think of when there's trouble there.'

'I had nowt to do with it. Besides, didn't you find –'

'What?' Gunter said quickly. And when Merrick, biting his lip, made no reply, he went on: 'Did you expect us to find something at the scene, Tom?'

'I don't know what you mean.'

'It's a pity you don't have anyone to corroborate your alibi, lad. Looks bad – two barns go up in flames and you doing all you can to make trouble for N.Y. Estates by running a protest meeting against them.'

'I ... I can corroborate my alibi. I forgot. Jack Sugden were with me doing the chairs. It slipped my mind.'

'Did it now. You should take one of those memory improvement courses, Tom.' Gunter shrugged. 'Well, you're in luck, because Jack Sugden says you were with him, and we've no reason to disbelieve him. So that puts you in the clear, doesn't it?'

'So can I go?'

'It puts him in the clear too, Tom. That's a funny thing, isn't it? Without his statement you might be in the soup.'

'I haven't got any time to stand around listening to your yarns, Mr Gunter. I'd like to get home.'

'You do that, lad, you do that. And remember if you put a foot wrong, I'll have you back in front of the court taking your porridge so fast you'll make a scorch mark on the way.'

Merrick left the police station in a state of baffled anger. The whole thing had gone wrong. It had looked foolproof – for who had more reason to cause trouble to N.Y. Estates than Jack Sugden, a man who was always criticising their farming methods in public. Resentful and perplexed, Merrick went home.

His wife heard about the fire and Jack's encounter with the police when Sandie came in from spending the evening with a friend in Beckindale. She was breathless with news.

'What d'you think?' she cried.

'You beat Jill Spencer at snakes and ladders?' her brother suggested.

'We played chess, so there!'

'Oh, very intellectual,' said Jackie. 'Though mating isn't all to do with brains.'

'Jackie!' his mother reproved sharply. 'Sandie wanted to tell us something.'

Sandie paused before exploding the bombshell. 'Jack Sugden was arrested for setting fire to a barn at Ridge Farm!'

Pat's reaction was immediate. 'Don't be silly, Sandie! Who ever told you such a lie?'

'It's true!' Sandie cried. 'Jill's father came back from the meeting and told us all about it. The police came and took him away right in the middle of it.'

Even Jackie was astonished. 'Set fire to a barn?'

'Two barns, in fact. Mr Spencer said you could see the blaze from Beckin Bridge.'

Pat had jumped up and grabbed her coat. 'I'm going to phone Emmerdale,' she said.

'But there's nothing you can do, is there?'

'That's not the point, Jackie. I want to know what's happening.'

'Take the torch,' he reminded her as she stepped out, feeling for coins for the box. When the door had closed he shook his head. 'Can't believe Jack Sugden would set fire to a barn.'

'That's not all I heard,' Sandie said.

'What else? He robbed a bank too?'

'It's serious, Jackie. Jill asked me if it was true my Mum had decided to get a divorce and marry Jack Sugden.'

'Who the hell told her that?' Jackie exclaimed, his young face darkening.

'Don't swear, Jackie. You know Mum doesn't like it. And as for who told her . . . Jill said Dad had been in a pub telling everybody about it.'

'Oh, they say that kind of thing about him –'

144

'Did you ask her . . . you know, when you said you were going to? Whether we were going to go back with Dad?'

'Yeh . . .'

'What did she say?'

'She . . . she just said he was no good. She said she . . . couldn't go back to him. I dunno what she meant.'

Sandie looked at him. Boys were so dense. . . . It was no use trying to explain it to him.

Pat's phone call interrupted an anxious discussion between Annie, Matt and Dolly. Annie went to pick up the receiver, and was unable to give Pat any helpful information.

'Nay, lass, all we know he's been asked to answer some questions. Arrested? Of course not!' She was shocked. 'Folk have got hold of t'wrong end of t'stick. Henry Wilks has gone after him to the police station, just to see what's to do, but it can't be anything, Pat.'

'Will you let me know what happens?'

'He'll probably come and tell you all about it himself, love. Don't you worry about it.' She put down the phone and went back to the fireside. 'She seems right upset,' she said.

Dolly exchanged a glance with Matt. 'Aye,' she said, 'I suppose she is.'

'She said her daughter brought the news home. I suppose it's all over t'village.'

'Has to be,' Matt sighed. 'It happened right in front of everybody.'

'Oh, aye, Amos could hardly wait to get to a phone,' Dolly reminded him. 'He never expected quite so big a scoop when he came to the meeting.'

Amos had been quite beside himself when he came into the Woolpack. He was making exclamations in headlines: 'Meeting in Uproar! Surprise Incident Happens! Famous Author Arrested!'

'Arrested?' Seth inquired. 'Who got arrested?'

'Jack Sugden, Famous Beckindale Author!' Amos told him. 'Taken From Meeting!'

'Taken? Handcuffed, tha means?'

'Police Escort Him! Platform Speakers Silenced!'

Amos was trying to dial the number of the *Hotten Courier* with fingers that trembled. Nothing so exciting had happened in Beckindale since the Woolpack had a break-in, and this was more enjoyable because he wasn't in any personal danger.

The value of this 'scoop' was somewhat diminished when Jack Sugden himself walked in with Henry Wilks about an hour later. 'Hello, Jack,' Seth said. 'Thought you'd be in a suit wi' arrows on it by now.'

'Are you still doing the honours?' Jack said. 'Because if so, I'll have a large pint, and Henry will have a whisky.'

'Celebrating your freedom?' Seth said, obliging.

'Recovering my sanity, more like. Fancy thinking I'd set fire to a barn!'

'They must have had some reason, though,' Amos put in with anxiety. He didn't want the value of his news to be totally demolished.

'Oh, aye, they had summat they thought of as evidence. Some chap had pinched a handkerchief of mine and dropped it near the barn. But I was able to convince 'em it went missing three or four days ago.'

'Fancy that,' Seth said.

Amos went to telephone the latest state of play. His editor said crossly: 'Don't keep ringing with corrections, Amos. Wait till you get the correct story and let me have it. After all, it's missed this week's press date. It doesn't have to be put into print for five days.'

Dashed, Amos went back to his bar, to find Seth leaning there in splendour taking up all the room.

'Thank you, Seth,' he said stiffly. 'Now that I'm back on duty, there's no need for you to stay.'

'Oh, but thee's busy, Amos. Look at t'crowd.'

'I can manage. Any road, it'll soon be closing time.'

'Tell thee what,' Seth said, 'so long as Henry's having this holiday at Emmerdale, you can rely on me to give you a hand in t'bar any time you want. I take to it – I think I've got a talent for it.'

'The need isn't likely to arise, thanks, Seth.'

'But if you've got another important event to cover as a reporter, Amos –'

'I'll manage.' The truth was, Amos didn't really like having Seth in a position of privilege. He had an uneasy feeling that he would end up a loser. The minute the Woolpack was closed he intended to do a balance of cash in the till against spirits sold – and he had a dreadful suspicion he'd find quite a quantity of whisky and brandy unaccounted for.

'I think they liked having me here, Amos,' Seth insisted. 'I think I've got the personality for it.'

'I think there's quite enough of that kind of thing with me here,' Amos said, stern and unyielding. ''Sides, I never asked you to put in any personality – just to serve drinks.'

'You ask your customers. They'll tell thee they enjoyed having me here.'

'I'll do no such thing! I don't have to ask my customers for their opinion.'

'Market research, that's called, Amos. It'd improve the place no end if you found out what they preferred –'

'Seth Armstrong, I don't need any advice from you on how to run my business! I'll be glad if you'll step from behind that bar and take your proper place as a customer.'

'Huh!' Seth said. 'You were glad enough to have me stand in for you when you wanted to get away –'

'Don't flatter yourself, lad! I couldn't get anybody else.'

'There's gratitude for thee! You're just put out because folk liked having somebody agreeable.'

'Agreeable's a matter of opinion, and I'll thank you to leave me to run my business as I think fit. If you can't keep your notions to yourself, go elsewhere for your beer, Seth Armstrong.'

Seth drew himself up and pulled the peak of his knitted gamekeeper's cap down to meet his thick brows. 'Right, an' I will,' he said. 'Just you wait and see. I'll be missed here!'

He stalked out, leaving Amos speechless at such conceit.

The tiff lasted through into Monday. Seth had business in Hotten but would normally have hurried back so as to have his usual lunchtime pint at the Woolpack. But to spite Amos he went into the Red Lion in Golden Lane in Hotten. Just to show he was totally emancipated, he bought himself a glass of imported German lager. He didn't really like it, but he intended to tell Amos it was infinitely preferable to the Monks' dark ale that Amos supplied.

Along the bar was a short, thin figure in four sweaters and a muffler. 'Hello, Seth,' he said.

'Hello, Whippy. Here's your health.'

'Aye, and yours. What's that you're drinking?'

'It's lager.'

'I'll try one.' Whippy sought about in the pockets of his sweaters, coming out with a small handful of pound notes.

'Hey-up!' Seth exclaimed, brushing lager froth off his forked moustache. 'You won the pools?'

'Nay, lad.' Whippy laid one finger drunkenly alongside his nose. 'I did a little job for a frien' . . . got paid for my trouble.'

'So I see. Nice to see some folk know how to make money.'

'Aye,' Whippy agreed, 'an' put a spoke in the wheels of them as thinks they can push other folk around.' He waved at the bartender. 'Willie, another o' them that Seth's got.'

'I don't mind if I do,' Seth said, finishing his lager in haste. 'But make mine half of bitter, Willie.'

Whippy Barton looked puzzled at this turn of events, but grinned when Seth urged him to explain his sudden excess of wealth.

'Nobody can say I ever refused a favour to a friend,' he declared, 'and Tom Merrick's always been a friend of mine.'

'Tom Merrick?' Seth repeated, his eyebrows going up.

148

Whippy winked. 'They had him in about it,' he whispered loudly. 'But they couldn't hold him, could they? He wasn't anywhere near the fire.'

'The fire? At Ridge Farm?'

The bartender put Whippy's lager in front of him. He picked up the slender glass, took a deep swallow, then glared at Seth. 'Why d'you recommend this stuff to me?' he inquired in a vexed tone. 'Tastes like Dettol!'

'Have a bitter, Whippy. On me,' said Seth, willing to spend money in a good cause.

'Nay, lad, nay – I'm the one with the money,' Whippy replied. 'Willie, pint of best!'

'So Tom Merrick gave you all that, did he?'

'All that, and more. Ten quid ... should have asked more, really. Didn't realise how big it was all going to be when it got going ... Still, when you've agreed a price, 's a matter of honour to stick to it, isn't it.'

'Right you are, Whippy. So Tom Merrick asked you to set fire to N.Y.'s barns, did he?'

'I never said that!' Whippy shouted. 'Who says I said that?'

'Here, you,' said the barman, putting a pint in front of him, 'you pipe down or it's out!' He jerked a broad thumb at the door.

Whippy cowered back, took a swig at his beer, then peered at Seth. 'It's a dead secret,' he said. 'Secret as the grave ... But I don't mind you knowin' because we're old friends and you prevented me drinking that funny foreign ale. Aye, you and me, Seth. Remember when we took them pheasants at Stonor Park and sold 'em in Loudwick to the cook from the great house?'

'Nay, that weren't me, Whippy ... Any more than it was thee that set that fire at Ridge Farm.'

Whippy winked. 'But nobody paid us to take them pheasants. That was private enterprise.'

'I don't believe you got ten quid from Tom Merrick. Where'd he get that kind of money?'

'Dunno. An' I've not much left, that's a fact. Still, it was good while it lasted. Ten quid ... Good ol' Tom.'

'Aye,' Seth said in a quiet voice, 'good old Tom.' He

had his own opinion of good old Tom. He was pretty sure Pat Merrick had been talking about Tom when he saw her being led by Jack Sugden to his Land-Rover, her face all beaten and bruised. Her husband had beaten her up. And because she turned to Jack for help, Merrick had set a trap for him, to get him accused of arson. Seth had heard about the initialled handkerchief: he had no idea how either Merrick or Whippy Barton could have got hold of it but he had no doubt Whippy had planted it at the fire to incriminate Jack.

He got back to Home Farm soon after one. Richard Anstey had asked to see him during Anstey's lunch hour. He found him on the telephone in the study, looking anxious.

'Yes, sir, I understand it looks like a campaign. You may be right, someone may be running it on purpose. Yes, I will, I'll look into it. I'll report back.'

Seth had come in while this conversation went on. He stood quietly just inside the door. Richard looked up to find him observing him. 'Oh, there you are, Seth. Listen, we've got to start on an economy drive straight away. What with one thing and another, the company's had a lot of unexpected losses this winter here at Beckindale.'

'Aye, that's a fact, what with Christmas trees stolen and barns going on fire –'

'And protest meetings over footpaths making illwill –'

Seth nodded, looking down. He hadn't quite intended his little ploy about the footpath to end the way it did.

'You were asking for a thousand pheasant chicks to make good the shortage of pheasants for next season's shooting . . . '

'Aye, that's right, Mr Anstey. If there's to be enough to make decent bags for the shooting parties, we've got to replace the deficiencies.'

'Well, we can't. You'll have to make do with five hundred.'

'Five hundred?' Seth said, shocked. 'But Mr Anstey, them few'll hardly be enough to make wings in t'sky!'

'I can't help it. We haven't the money. And I can tell you this. If we have any more mishaps that cost us money, we may have to dispense with pheasant rearing entirely for a season.'

'But that would mean cancelling almost all the shoots,' said Seth, picturing the loss of tips that would mean. Good bags for the guns meant good tips for gamekeepers.

'That's the way it has to be. So I'll be cutting down your funds for the pheasant rearing.'

'I can't manage wi' so few chicks, Mr Anstey.'

'You'll have to.'

They argued it back and forth until at last Seth wrung from Anstey a promise that he would see if funds would run to seven hundred and fifty. It was a partial victory. But it was one more thing to ponder when Seth went home to his late midday meal.

Still in a pet with Amos, Seth went to the Maltshovel that evening. Tom Merrick was there, alone, at the corner of the bar. Seth took up a spot at the far end.

'Being stand-offish, are you?' Merrick inquired in a surly manner.

'Nay, I came in for a bit of peace and quiet,' Seth said. He ordered his drink without troubling to move any nearer to Merrick. By and by the bar filled up somewhat and Merrick became the centre of a little crowd. He was still something of a local hero, the man who had organised the protest meeting about the footpath. True, the meeting had been wrecked by the removal of Jack Sugden by the police but that didn't lessen Merrick's prestige as a leader of public opinion.

'If you ask me,' Merrick said, 'they came and dragged him out just so as to spoil our meeting and make us get in a muddle. That Mr Anstey brought the police, didn't he?'

'Aye, so he did. You're right, lad.'

'An' I'll tell you another thing,' Merrick said, in a loud, hectoring voice. 'I wouldn't be surprised to hear that N.Y. Estates set those barns on fire themselves.'

'What? Oh, come on.' It was a chorus of disbelief.

'Well, you just think about it. Who stands to gain by it?'

'Nobody.'

'Don't you believe it, lads! Them barns was well insured, you can bet on it. And so they get their money back, don't they? An' they make it look as if one o' us did it out of spite, so we look bad and they look hard done by. Am I right?'

'Right!' chorused his audience.

Seth finished his beer and went out. There were times when it was hard to be a man of peace. He would dearly have loved to take a coop stave to Tom Merrick.

Chapter Thirteen

When the insurance assessor arrived to look at the fire wreckage at Ridge Farm he was accompanied by one of the N.Y directors, Mr Duparc. 'What a mess,' Duparc muttered. 'Have the police any idea who did it?'

Richard Anstey shrugged. 'I get the feeling they have a fair suspicion but no proof.'

'Wasn't there some talk of a clue left on the scene, though?' Robinson of Farm and Country Insurance inquired.

'Yes, a handkerchief. It appears it was a clumsy attempt to incriminate someone who had a perfect alibi. A grudge plot, perhaps.'

'Someone seems to have a grudge against N.Y. Estates,' Robinson said. 'Our local man tells us there's a rumour going round that you started the fire yourself to get the insurance money.'

Duparc looked shocked. 'That's slander!'

'Of course. But it's the kind of thing that will be said if you're unpopular.' And he gazed at the NY director. 'And it seems you are unpopular.'

'What are you saying?' grunted Duparc, getting out a cigar and fiddling with it to cover his anxiety.

'I'm saying that, while our company will of course meet your claim on this fire, your premiums will have to go up considerably to meet the risk implied by the bad feeling in the neighbourhood. What's happened once can happen again.'

'Oh, Lord,' Duparc groaned, and lit his cigar to comfort himself.

Afterwards, when the insurance assessor had been given a whisky and sent on his way, Duparc looked with some sternness at Anstey. 'We can't afford this illwill,' he said. 'It's costing us direct money! The main cause at the moment is this footpath, isn't it?'

'I'm afraid so, sir, but the board's instructions –'

'The board reconsidered it at our last planning meeting. We had a letter from a shareholder complaining of the plan and saying he intended to raise it at the Annual Meeting with some hopes that the newspaper reporters would take it up.'

'Oh, no!'

'No, precisely. The last thing we want is uproar at the shareholders' meeting with the press there. So we've decided to put the matter off for the time being.'

Anstey half-smiled. 'Shall I let the village know?'

'Sooner the better. And we'll write to this shareholder and tell him our decision. By the way, he's a local man . . . Er . . . the name eludes me . . . He wrote from the local inn, which I presume he runs . . . '

'Was the name Henry Wilks?'

'That was it.'

'I see,' Anstey said, and turned aside to hide his grin. The sly old devil! Bought some shares, did he? Only so as to write and complain as a shareholder . . . Well, it had worked.

Joe passed on the news to Henry a few hours later when he called in at Emmerdale. 'Mr Duparc was really bothered, Henry, by a letter he'd got from some shareholder threatening action at the shareholders' meeting.'

'Oh aye,' Henry said, deadpan. 'Shareholders can be an awful nuisance – I know, because they use to make speeches when I ran a business and was trying to run a quiet meeting.'

'There you are then. Some interfering busybody has put a spoke in N.Y.'s wheel.'

'Fancy that.' Henry let a moment pass then said, 'Joe, have you heard this gossip that's going round the village about Jack and Pat Merrick?'

'Oh, there's always gossip—'

'But this time they're saying they got it direct from Tom Merrick. Merrick says Pat's started divorce proceedings because she wants to marry Jack.'

'Does she, by heck!'

'He hasn't mentioned it to you?'

Joe shook his head. Then after a moment he said, 'You know Tom Merrick. Anything to be a pest, especially to a man who befriends his wife ... '

'True enough. But it could mean big changes here, Joe,' Henry said, nodding to the farmhouse gleaming in the cold sunlight of a March afternoon, seen like a toy from the slopes of Grey Top Field.

'So it could, Henry ... ' They considered it for a moment. 'What does Ma say?'

'She doesn't know. She doesn't get down to the village as much just at present because of her knee. But it'll get to her sooner or later.'

As it happened, it was considerably sooner. After the evening meal, when everyone else had gone out, Henry and Annie were left alone. 'Well, Henry, what's the secret?' Annie demanded.

'Secret?'

'Matt and Dolly know summat—they've been avoiding my eye the last couple of days. And Amos rang me up this afternoon, asking the daftest questions.'

'About what?'

'Well, about our Jack, it seemed like, but you know how hard it is to get any sense out of Amos.' She hesitated, her eyes troubled. 'Is Jack in any trouble over this fire business, because of the hankie? I thought Sergeant MacArthur seemed quite satisfied with my answers when he spoke to me about it.'

'It's not the fire, Annie.'

'Then what?'

Henry fiddled with the cup he was supposed to be drying. 'Well ... I don't like to ...'

'Is it something you've been told in confidence?' Annie sat down, watching him.

'No. In fact, it's general gossip and you'll hear it sometime, I suppose, so I may as well ... The talk in the village is that Jack and Pat will get wed when she has her divorce.' He set the cup down on the dresser with care then turned to look at her.

To his surprise she merely nodded with complete calm. 'I can't see that's owt to worry about, Henry.'

'Is that all you have to say?' He was astonished.

'What else can I say? They're adults, fully capable of making up their own minds. Only ... I'd have liked to hear of it from Jack, if it's going to happen.'

'Aye,' Henry said heavily.

When they had finished the washing-up Henry said he thought he'd walk down to the Woolpack to soothe Amos's anxieties; he didn't want him spreading the rumour any further. By and by Jack came in to collect his jacket before completing his nightly tour of the lambing pens. 'Jack, bide a minute,' his mother said.

'Eh? I can't, really, Ma. It'll be dark soon.'

'I just want to ask you summat.'

'What's that, Ma?'

She took a breath. 'Are you going to marry Pat Merrick?'

Her son folded his jacket over his arm. 'Oh,' he murmured. 'So you've heard that, have you?'

'Seems everbody has heard it except me, lad.'

'Nay, I was late on the list myself. I didn't know about it until Amos cornered me soon after the Woolpack closed at dinnertime. He was all agog about it.'

'And where had he heard it?'

'From Tom Merrick, indirectly. But you can be sure of one thing, if Amos has heard it, everybody has.'

'Is it true?'

Jack gave a half-shake of the head. 'I'll tell you summat, Ma. Until I got the drift of Amos's questions, I'd never thought about it.' He turned to the door. 'I never thought of it ... till now.'

He went out to join Matt and Dolly for their walk to look

155

at the ewes. On his way he fell in with Seth Armstrong, out on the track of a fox who had been alarming the pheasants in the pens. 'Howdo, lad,' Seth said. 'Light's almost gone. You looking at your sheep?'

'Aye.'

'Foxes are always interested in newborn lambs, tha knows. But I'll get this beggar, don't fret.'

'I'm not fretting about that, Seth.'

'Summat else worrying thee?'

Jack shrugged and shook his head. 'Just the general awkwardness of the world in general, and Tom Merrick in particular.'

'Aye, lad, he's cost N.Y. Estates a packet, one way or t'other.'

'Huh! If it was only money . . .'

'Oh, he could cost jobs too. Mr Anstey says as they're going to have to economise to cover costs incurred by having to put a watch on the barns for fear of the fire-raiser . . .'

They stood for a moment in silence, reviewing the havoc caused by Tom Merrick. Jack was too involved with his own personal problems to notice how Seth had linked Merrick with the fire-raising. Then Seth bestirred himself. 'Well, I'd better get on. See you some time, Jack.'

'Aye, Seth.'

During the long night hours while he kept watch for the fox, Seth Armstrong did some deep thinking. The result was that next day, when he had had a nap and seen to routine chores, he went to Hotten on the bus. There he drifted from one pub to another until, in the fullness of time, he ran across Merrick having lunch – a pint of dark ale and a pork pie.

'How do, Tom,' Seth said, sitting down uninvited at the same table.

'Who asked you to sit there?' Tom growled. He was in a bad temper. He had a hangover, all his plans seemed to have misfired, and he was running short of cash.

'You'll be pleased I did when you hear what I have to

say, lad. I'm sitting here because I'm worried about your health.'

'You what?' Merrick said through a mouthful of pie.

'Aye, right worried about you, I am. I don't think this neighbourhood's healthy for you.'

'Don't talk so daft. I've lived here all my life and never been ill –'

'But it'd make you a bit sick, wouldn't it, if you felt the sergeant's hand on your collar? It'd mean right into jail to serve them twelve months they awarded you.'

Merrick put down the rest of the pie and stared at Seth. 'What you on about?'

'Well, I'll tell you, but first I'll have to have a drink otherwise my throat'll be too dry to say much.'

'Well, go and get one!'

'What, when it's because of you I'm so worried my mouth's gone dry?'

Merrick glared at him. But then, after a moment while they looked at each other eye to eye, he rose slowly and went to the bar, where he bought a half for Seth. Seth watched him, a smile hidden behind his moustache.

'There, that's all you get – and five minutes of my time.'

Seth sampled the beer and nodded. Then, as if starting a new topic, he said: 'Had an interesting conversation wi' a mate of yours, Tom. Whippy Barton.'

He watched the other man go tense. 'Whippy? He don't usually talk much.'

'Only when he's steeped. And he were steeped that night, 'cos somebody had given him a lot of money. Ten quid, he said.'

Now Merrick was watching Seth's every move. 'Aye?' he said.

'Seems he did this friend a favour. A big favour, eh? — to be worth a tenner.'

Merrick swallowed hard. 'What's this got to do wi' me?'

'Thought you'd be interested to hear that Whippy was so conversational, since he's a pal o' yours.'

'Huh! Some pal,' Merrick growled.

157

'What I was thinking was this ... Suppose Sergeant MacArthur was to get conversational wi' Whippy? I mean, it could happen. And you never know what MacArthur might find out.'

'I couldn't care less.'

'That's good. I'm glad you're not worried about it. 'Cos it seems to me you've enough to be worried about. For instance, a man that raises his fist to a woman can't have many friends.'

'What're you talking about?'

'I was by when your missus was taken to hospital by Jack Sugden. And you know, she were begging him not to make her go to t'police 'cos it would mean some feller might have to go straight into clink. I was pretty sure she meant thee, Tom Merrick. Funny, that. The same thing applies to this feller Whippy was rabbitin' on about. If it ever came out that he'd paid a man to ... well, to do summat bad ... that's a crime, tha knows. Conspiracy, or summat.'

Merrick could contain his rage no longer. 'Are you threatening me, Seth Armstrong?'

'Me? Threaten a man as has bought me a drink? Nay, lad, I'd never do that. It's Whippy you want to worry about. He may be close-mouthed as a rule, but when he's got a drop in him he rambles on a lot. And you know, detectives have a lot of friends among pub-keepers – they pick up a lot from chatting to 'em.'

Seth looked hopefully at his empty mug. Merrick said: 'I'm not buying any more so don't expect it. You're trying to scare me out o' my own home town.'

'I'm tryin' to do thee a favour, lad. I'm tryin' to tell thee, tha's not nearly as clever as tha thinks. You don't see how the climate round here has changed – I'm sure it could damage your health, like cigarettes.'

'Mind your own business!'

'Right.' Seth got to his feet slowly and nodded a farewell. 'So long, Tom. I hope next time I hear of thee, it's not from a newspaper report that the law's taken its course ... Sad, that'd be. But happen inevitable if you close your ears to good sense.'

With his slow, unhurried stride, Seth left the Red Lion. He felt he had done as much as he could to rid the neighbourhood of a pest as troublesome as the fox he'd missed last night.

Jack Sugden came to Hotten later the same day, but since the pubs were closed he knew he had better look for Merrick at the flat he shared with Derek Warne. It was Warne who opened the door to him, in stockinged feet and with his shirt tail hanging out. 'What d'you want?' he grunted, annoyed at being wakened from his afternoon nap.

'Is Tom Merrick in? Can I have a word?'

'What about?' Warne said, suddenly cagey.

'It's personal,' Jack replied. He wanted to ask Merrick why he'd started the rumour about the marriage between him and Pat, and whether or not he was going to co-operate in the matter of Pat's divorce.

'You're not the law?' Jack shook his head. 'In that case, I don't mind telling you. He's cleared out.'

'Cleared out? You mean for good?'

'Looks like it. He came back from the pub this afternoon in a flaming temper, said some goon had threatened him. I dunno what it was all about, but he threw his stuff into a suitcase and scarpered.' Warne scratched his head. 'Now I come to think on it, he went without paying me his rent! He's supposed to go halves ... By heck, he owed me for the last week as well!'

'Do you know where he went?'

'No, if I did I'd go after him and get that fourteen quid!' He eyed Jack. 'You wouldn't care to stump up for him, would you, since you seem to be a friend of his?'

'I'm no friend of Tom Merrick's,' Jack said in a cool tone. 'Quite the reverse, in fact. You're sure you don't know where he's gone? Or when he's coming back?'

'I doubt if he'll be back. I was a bit sozzled but I'm sure I heard him say that what with his marriage going bad on him and one thing and the other, he was finished with Hotten. He was moaning about the divorce, saying that if she wanted it she might as well have it and put an end to everything. *I* said, 'What about the kids?' 'cos he seemed to keep a hold on the boy . . . what's his name . . . Jackie. An' all he said was, 'She can have 'em'. So I don't think he'll be back.'

Jack hesitated, then nodded. 'Thanks,' he said. 'Go back to your snooze.'

'Thanks for nothing,' Warne said, and slammed the door.

Jack drove back to Beckindale with a thousand thoughts crowding through his head. With Merrick gone, life would be so much simpler and happier for Pat. True, the children would still be a worry, particularly Jackie who seemed to have a lot of loyalty and affection for his Dad. But in time, perhaps, the lad would get over it.

If, in fact, Merrick was Jackie's father. Once again Jack turned the question over in his mind. Jackie could be his own boy – everything fitted, both as to the time of his birth and the kind of character he had. But Pat had never said anything on that score.

Well, of course she wouldn't . . . It would be like trying to make some claim on Jack. She would never do that. No matter what the gossips said, Pat had never so much as breathed a word about a future to be shared with Jack. She had scrupulously avoided giving the impression that she expected anything from him.

For that he admired her. He had a deep, steady affection for her. Whether it was more than that he wasn't sure – whether it would ever return to the passion he had once felt in years gone by . . . All he knew was that he enjoyed being with her more than with any other woman, even the clever and beautiful women he had met in the film business in Rome.

Well, there was no hurry. She had yet to set the divorce process in motion. And even when that was done, it would take her some time to get back her emotional balance after the life she'd led with Tom Merrick.

But by and by . . . By and by, who could tell? The idea of confounding all the gossips by actually marrying Pat made him smile.

Or perhaps something else made him smile – the feeling that the future held something good and precious in store.